Stolen Beauty
The B&D Chronicles

Piper St. James

ISBN 978-1-912768-52-3

Published 2019

Published by Black Velvet Seductions Publishing

Stolen Beauty Copyright 2019 Piper St. James
Cover design Copyright 2019 Jessica Greeley

Dedication

For J.S.,

The most understanding Dominant and Mentor in the world. You saw something in me no one else had ever recognized before—potential. Everything I lacked in my childhood, adolescence, and young adult life, I found in you: structure, support, discipline, and unconditional love. My teacher, my pillar of strength, my Dominant.

Without your encouragement, I would never have put pen to paper to create anything worth a damn. Even more so, without your guidance I would be nothing. I wouldn't be worth anything to anyone, first and foremost to myself.

For M.M.,

The man who released my primal huntress. You took a chance on this blue-eyed girl with an insatiable passion for hedonism, something she didn't even know existed within herself until we met! I will always be forever grateful to you for bringing out my inner switch, as well as your sense of adventure and creativity, which compliments my own.

Lastly, I owe you my deepest and sincerest gratitude for that first night you approached me to introduce yourself. Without that, none of our adventures would exist, nor would this book have been written.

Prologue

Her phone had chirped with the text message invite about an hour ago. It was the address for a pop-up bondage club at a warehouse downtown. Excitement coursed through her from head to toe as her eyes scanned the message to re-read it again and again.

She recognized the address vaguely, enough to know it was in a bad part of the city. She bit her lip anxiously as she checked the address on her computer just to be sure. Her initial assumption about the location was right, and her teeth bit down a little deeper. Admittedly, part of the thrill was leaving her posh middle-class apartment to venture into the city at night, but she couldn't ignore the voice in the back of her head that told her to be cautious.

Pop-up fetish clubs were the new raves—a vacant and abandoned warehouse one evening, the site of a killer bondage club the next, then back to a warehouse by the time the sun rose the next morning. The patrons valued their clubs, so there usually weren't any signs of the activities from the night before.

She had attended these parties before, and she always had a great time. The city was a place she had been warned about since childhood —the fetish clubs and the old ways of the world were less refined than their own—but it added to the excitement of doing something so taboo. She and her friends must have been to a dozen parties over the years, maybe more. However, it was always with her usual group of friends that she attended, and tonight none of them were available to go.

Unfortunately for her, tonight some of them were out of town or on dates, while others had just ghosted her invite. Typical. While they were indeed her friends, most were entitled bitches that she just kept around for appearance's sake. Petty, yes, but this was the way her class of luxury and money lived and operated on the secondary tier.

The fact that none of them were available to go to this party made her hesitate as her finger lingered over the confirmation of her RSVP on her phone. Sure, she could take a car down to the city by herself ... but should she? She had never gone into the city solo, but tonight she was in dire need of some fun, and this club was calling her name.

Fuck it. She confirmed her reservation on her mobile, and that was that! She chose one of her favorite outfits—a short black vinyl skirt with matching bra. They were shiny and smooth, and in the light they glistened like slick oil against her tan skin. The lack of a shirt openly exposed her golden necklace that bared her initial, a lower-case "y."

Her shoes were silver glitter platforms—not the most efficient to dance in, but they gave her an additional four inches of height. She would silently tolerate the pain if they made her look that much taller.

She was going to paint her nails, but she didn't have the time or patience, and her makeup received the same minimal treatment. She knew she was beautiful without it, and she had the confidence not to spend hours in front of the mirror to make herself up before going out. Maybe it was more than confidence, bordering on ego, but basic foundation, some soft pink lipstick, and mascara was all she applied. She brushed her bubblegum-pink bob haircut, roughly the same shade as her lips, and was ready to go.

***

By the time she arrived at the fetish club, it was in full swing. She always knew how to time an entrance.

Various bondage scenes were already set up and underway, scattered throughout the open play space. In the far end of the warehouse, a makeshift stage was assembled, with speakers pumping trance music to a crowd of eccentric dancers. Retro seemed to be in this season. The song changed to what she recognized as a remix from the group Daft Punk from nearly fifty years ago, maybe more. The crowd went up in a cheer at the first indication of the song, and broke into an energy that matched the music's rhythm.

Some of the club goers were holding plastic cups, while others danced with glow sticks and hula hoops that came to life with LEDs. Radiant pinks, greens, oranges, and yellows all lit up the crowd. Many were in bondage gear, including collars, harnesses, and fishnet clothing that was either traditional black or obnoxiously loud neon, while others were wearing nothing at all.

The music swirled and intermixed with the scenes of pain and pleasure all around her. It made her feel alive in a way nothing else did in this world, and it all created a natural high that she coasted on in her head. Embracing the adrenaline being released along her limbs and the dopamine in her brain, she realized this is why she ventured into the city at tonight alone. This is what she lived for.

She found a place along the wall where she could watch a scene with a few other gathering spectators. A tall Amazon beauty with golden skin and long black hair was in control of her bottom, another woman with a shaggy blonde pixie haircut streaked with wisps of pink and teal. She was chained from a rig that was suspended from the ceiling. It was raised just enough that the petite woman had to stand on the balls of her feet—nearly her tiptoes—in order to avoid hanging from her wrists. Her slim, naked body was stretched out, vulnerable to her tormentor.

The Amazon stalked around her prey. The young bottom had her eyes squeezed shut in anticipation, and a slight bit of dread at the oncoming sting of whatever implement her Mistress chose to use on her exposed skin made her bottom lip tremble. Y could feel the buzz amongst the crowd as they watched the scene unfold in front of them.

The Amazon's black leather boots, stretching up to her knees, clicked on the concrete floor. They were far enough from the music that even the audience could hear her calculated footfalls. The beautiful Top wore skinny jeans, accentuating her beautiful ass, and a black halter top. Her slender yet powerful arms were covered in ink that crawled along her skin and surely worked its way down her back.

Her confidence spoke volumes, and she didn't need flashy club wear to impress others or communicate her stature in the scene or the experience she harnessed. A flick of her raven hair and a curl of her lips as she stalked her prey made each and every spectator want to be beneath her, or crave to Top her. Y had seen this beauty before at the dungeons, and she knew this one would never, ever yield beneath another.

She brought the whip that was in her hand over her bottom's right breast with uncanny accuracy. It struck its target, kissing the flesh and leaving its mark upon the supple skin. The restrained girl yipped, and sadistic smiles spread throughout the crowd. Another quick lash from the whip struck, this time hitting her on the left butt cheek, making her almost lose the footing she struggled so desperately to keep.

Across the room, Y met eyes with another spectator. He was tall, clad in leather pants and matching shirt with combat boots. He was the definition of "tall, dark, and handsome," with eyes that were always on her as she moved hers coyly away and then back to him.

This could be fun, she thought as she separated herself from the group, seeing if her watcher would follow her. As she made her way away from the crowd, she definitely felt someone in her peripheral vision moving alongside her a few dozen feet away. She grinned to herself, thinking how she'd successfully baited her handsome suitor.

The problem with clubs like this was there weren't many places to be alone, unless you wanted to brave the rest of the warehouse, which was usually dilapidated and in shambles. However, there was usually one place in every warehouse that she could utilize.

She pushed a door open, leading to the fire escape. Fortunately there weren't any smokers on the metal landing at the moment, and she was able to be alone to see if her stalker would follow. She leaned on the railing, positioning herself in a coy and demure pose, trying to play innocent, with the intentions of ravaging him upon his entrance. A wolf in sheep's clothing.

The minutes crawled by. *Where was he?* She was beginning to get impatient, and that would soon lead to aggravation. Just as she was about to turn to go back inside, she heard the click of the door as it opened behind her. *Finally*, she thought to herself.

"It took you long enough." She grinned into the night air, still facing away from the door.

She felt his hand trace along the side of her body, warm and smooth against her skin, cool from the night's breeze. Suddenly his light caresses ceased and he grabbed her from behind, pulling her into him, yanking her back so hard her fingers slipped from the fire escape, her nails scratching the metal railing and making an awful noise.

Instinctively she tried to pull away and turn to face him, but she wasn't strong enough as the leather-gloved fingers dug into her arms. Something in her brain instantly knew this wasn't play. She was now prey. All of those stories about the dangers of the city flashed through her mind, and instantaneously she knew she was in trouble.

She kicked and struggled, trying to get out of his grasp. One of her platform shoes flew off in her attempts and clattered down the fire escape stairs, where it descended into the darkness beneath them.

The leather-clad hands moved to her throat where they began to squeeze, literally taking the breath from her before she could scream. She struggled fruitlessly as the grip tightened. She opened her mouth to yell for help, but all that came out were the last gurgles of air she had being pushed out of her lungs.

Her eyes went wide with fear and she desperately tried to claw at the hands that kept her captive. She could feel the adrenaline begin to fade from her muscles, and the lack of oxygen was closing in on her vision. She desperately tried to stay conscious, thinking if she struggled hard enough or stayed conscious long enough, someone would find them and help her. After what seemed like fifteen minutes of struggling and not being able to breathe, which realistically was probably less than a minute, she could feel herself slipping. Her muscles were becoming tired and her lungs screamed in pain. She was wrong; no one was coming for her. Suddenly everything went black and her fight was over.

Chapter One

Detective Wes Ellis rolled over in his bed. Red satin sheets were strewn aside, and his once brown hair, now long turning grey, was tousled from his sleep, or perhaps from the activities of earlier that night. He pressed the palm of his hand against his forehead tightly as he rolled away from the edge of the bed and onto his back. Next to him, he heard a small noise come from the twisted mess of a duvet and saw a mop of golden hair poking out from beneath it.

The night before slowly came back to him as his eyes wandered the floor on the opposite side of the bed. Bondage gear of all types was scattered across the bedroom beneath the highly raised bed. A spreader bar, various canes and crops, and a pair of heavy elkskin floggers all littered the hardwood floor. Smaller toys intermingled with the larger ones, including clover clamps, an o-ring gag, and vibrators ranging in all sizes, including a menacing-looking dildo. Last night had been a light affair because he knew he had to work the next morning, but they'd still made the most of it. *It was so rare their paths crossed these days*, he thought.

The stirring of the small noise from his side came again. He reached down to remove the blanket gently from his companion, who still slept peacefully at his side, and finally found her. Pulling back the blanket, he revealed a beautiful pale face, young and smooth. Luscious lips that had worn red lipstick the night before were now bare and gorgeous in their natural beauty. They slightly parted to release a small sigh as she slept.

In the puffy duvet cocoon, her features popped against the white fabric and gave her an angelic appearance. She looked so peaceful as she slept, so young and frozen in time. Removing more of the blanket, he revealed her slender shoulders, and that little sigh came again. It brought a smile to his lips. She was somewhere in that state between awake and asleep, where you could wake up with enough effort, but easily fall back into the dreamscapes you'd just left. He didn't want to disturb her, not just yet.

That crooked smile that had crossed his lips accompanied the amusement in his steel blue eyes as he admired the young woman, half his age, lying beside him. He continued to lower the blanket, now revealing her breasts that were once as pale as the rest of her, but were now swollen and held a bright, angry pink glow from the cane he had used last night to strike them. She had lain on her back, bound to the four posts of his king size bed. In this spread-eagle position, he was able to leave mark after mark, line after line, from his wooden cane.

Perfectly thin lines matched symmetrically on each breast. He admired his work for a moment before he completely removed the warm blanket she slumbered in. The cool morning air greeted her skin, and her nipples became perky and erect. They were no doubt sore to even the softest of touches.

He wanted to take one of them in his mouth this morning and suck on it as he had done the night before, then graze his teeth along the tip. This morning, even his breath would make them scream in pain, so to bite them would be a wonderful way to start the day for his lovely little masochist.

Watching her breasts rise and fall with each breath she took in her sleep, he remembered last night's events vividly. First, his fingers had caressed her gently, rolling her nipples between his fingertips until they became red, swollen, and hard. That was when they were the most ripe to bite, and that is exactly what he'd done. Her screams of ecstasy from the pain had only encouraged him to bite harder. She'd run her fingers through his hair and pulled, but this had not deterred him from his course. He would release, open his mouth wider, and envelop a mouthful of her soft breast with his teeth and bite down hungrily.

He bit her much more deeply than he would any other partner because he knew this one could take it—this one was different. He could have drawn blood and she would have gently pushed him away, tasted it on her fingertips, and then pulled him back to whisper in his ear to continue. This girl was special.

While that particularly deep bite mark made the left breast different from the right, still bearing his teeth marks this morning, they were nearly identical as she lay next to him. As his eyes traveled from her face and down her body, he could feel her body heat radiate against him. The scent of sex, sweat, and natural body pheromones escaped in a musky waft as lowered the blanket to the floor, fully revealing her naked body.

Her pussy was waxed and clean. Looking at it now only made his already hard cock ache with desire. Her thighs were covered in beautiful welts that would soon turn black and blue. They would then fade to a sickly yellowish green before their eventual departure from the skin.

Having played with her often enough, he knew these marks would only last five or six days maximum, and when he saw her again they would be long gone and he would have the pleasure of starting over again on a clean canvas. That is, if she hadn't found someone before him to leave new ones.

She was his go-to girl, what he considered his primary, but with the life he led, he didn't have as much time for her as he wanted, and certainly not as much as she deserved.

He also damned well knew he didn't deserve her. A man his age, currently kissing fifty years old on the ass next month, with a job that kept him away all hours of the day and night—he didn't deserve such a luxury. In fact, he was probably the last person worthy of her company.

She, however, was popular amongst the kink and polyamory circles alike. The fact she threw him a bone at all made him grateful. She could have anyone she wanted any day of the week, man or woman, and for all he knew, she did. But on their nights together she chose him, and hell if he knew why.

There had been many nights when he had requested her company and she had arrived with marks, both fresh and old, but he never asked about them and she never divulged their origin. Other times she would have cuts along her skin, some shallow and resembling scratches, others running deeper and still bandaged. Once again—don't ask, don't tell. It wasn't their way.

That was one of the cornerstones of their dynamic. Love had absolutely nothing to do with what they had; it was purely primal and sensual. They weren't indebted to each other in the slightest, and they didn't owe the other a single thing, let alone an explanation for the marks that graced her body. When they were together, it was their time to embrace the other's company—nothing else, and no one else, mattered.

He had on more than one occasion given her a mark from toys, blades, or teeth that left a long-lasting impression, and on very rare occasions a permanent mark of his own when she'd asked for it. However, through his experience and respect for her, he never left it in an obnoxiously obvious spot as untrained Tops and Dominants have been known to do.

Her creamy thighs, red and warm to the touch from the pain he'd bestowed upon her last night with a riding crop, led to her slender legs and perfectly manicured feet. Her toenails were painted red, as they always were, to match her fingernails. Red, in their world, meant many things—a safe word for "stop," a color they strived to turn the skin—but to her it was the color that made her look the most stunning and delicious when it adorned her body.

While catering to who knows how many other men and women, she always made him feel special. She always made him feel like he was the only one in the world that mattered to her—the mark of a great submissive.

Whenever she spent time with him, either out on the town or at his apartment, she knew what he liked and was happy to oblige. In his presence, she would wear either a blouse and pencil skirt, or a beautiful long dress with a slit up the right leg, revealing Cuban thigh-highs. The seams were always perfectly straight as they ran up the back of her legs, from her heel to just beneath her voluptuously round ass cheeks where they met the garter straps.

She'd be wearing heels, of course. It could be snowing, with three feet of snow already accumulated on the ground, and she would be navigating the sidewalks effortlessly in her stilettos. Her hair would either be up in loose curls, or straight and framing her delicate face. The two things that were always consistent were her red lips, and the golden necklace she wore bearing her first initial, a lower-case golden "c."

In their world, whenever someone wore such a necklace, it would either display the initial of their own name, or the name of their Owner. Tops displayed capital letters, while bottoms displayed lower case.

If it was their own name on the chain, this was an indication that the individual was not claimed, either by choice or by circumstance. However, if it was the initial of their Owner, they were off the market unless their Owner expressed otherwise.

Watching her as she slept, now he pondered this. He knew a lot about her. Actually, no, that was incorrect—he knew what she told him about herself. As a detective, he of all people knew that what people told you could be anything but the truth, so who knew if what she told him was just that? Yet to him it didn't matter; that was a luxury when you accepted the other at face value and didn't owe the other a thing. He didn't need the truth form her. Their relationship was purely physical, carnal, and indulgent.

What she had once told him was that she wasn't owned. She easily could have been, with her looks, experience, and skills. However, as she explained many times over when asked both by him and others in his company, that was not what she wanted. She wanted to be free and have experiences an Owner would never allow—experiences he or she would no doubt keep her from as a kept submissive. She wanted to be her own person. She wanted something that was an old-world concept—free will.

This was not a shared goal in their culture. In fact, it was extremely rare, since that meant she had to make her own way in the world, and their world was not always the safest place for a young, single female to be doing so. With his past caseload of victims, he should know better than anyone. Those who made their own way were usually in the lower ranks of society—the tertiary tier, as they called it. These citizens were ones who commonly led a life of prostitution and unsafe kink.

When he first met her, this was the most remarkable thing he had ever heard. A beautiful woman not wanting to be owned? Girls and boys from the age of eighteen who were submissive in nature begged to be owned, to be cared for and taken care of, to slave beneath one man or woman for the rest of their life. From their tenth birthday, they were trained in the ways to please prospective men and women.

No, not sexually, of course—not at such a young age. However, at ten they began their training in skills that every Owner would want in their bottom, the person who would serve beneath them. Education, culinary and domestic skills, how to hold and maintain proper conversation, as well as an array of very specific skill sets to cater to hobbies and interests their potential Owner may have and require of them, even if the bottom themselves had no personal interest. These were all valuable traits learned from their education structure, and, as you went up in the hierarchy, it only became stricter and more refined.

Ten years old may have seemed young to the world decades ago, if not centuries, but it appeared to be the age when the child would have an inkling if they leaned more toward the Dominant side or the submissive. Were they a Top or a bottom? Would they command others or be commanded?

Parents would take their children to a specialist in the field who would administer a scrutiny of psychological tests and come up with a result that would confirm or deny the child's own inner feelings. If the child came out as a switch, someone who enjoyed both Top and bottom experiences, they were shunned from being both and were forced to choose. If they refused, their parents would make the decision for them and their education would begin.

It was dangerous to be a switch, because it went against all of the rules their world had established. Men could be submissive and women could be Dominant, but never could one fall on both sides of the D/s slash, as they called it.

For a culture that was widely accepting of social and sexual ideas and ways of life that were once considered taboo in more repressed societies, being a switch was one of the greatest practices of the scene. However, Ellis had an inkling this was exactly what this girl sleeping beside him was. He'd assumed it the moment he'd laid eyes on her as he'd watched how she interacted with others at the bar they'd met at. She catered to some and ruled over others, but it was in the slightest and smallest of ways only a trained detective would be able to notice. The glint in her eye, a hand gesture, the guidance of walking half a step ahead or behind another, even her posture while sitting with someone spoke distinctly of her nature.

To the untrained eye she hid it well, but you can never really hide your true self from those who knew what to look for, and he knew exactly what those things were.

While her license said submissive, he didn't believe it. Not for a minute. There were other indicators too that went up like red flags that he mentally bookmarked as they continued to see each other.

For instance, when she came over and her skin was unblemished and clean, showing no indications of bruising, scoring, or marks of any kind, this was an extreme red flag. No way could someone who enjoyed receiving pain so much go so long without having any marks from receiving any. That is, not unless they enjoyed giving it as well.

He never questioned her unmarked skin; he could hear the excuses now, and, frankly, he didn't care. Somewhere deep down inside himself he knew her nature of being a switch was one of the things he enjoyed most about her. It made her unpredictable and extremely interesting, but he would never admit it to himself, let alone another person.

Hell, his job was taking these people who practiced both sides of the culture into holding to be evaluated. In their world, it was believed that when a person could not choose to be a Top or a bottom, this was an indication of a disturbed mind.

It seemed primitive and wrong, but he had seen far too many switches commit crimes to argue with the facts. However, that didn't mean many other disturbed minds who committed crimes every single day didn't identify on just one side of the slash. He had his suspicions that condemning switches was just the government's way of making the public feel safe from the prospects of living in an unpredictable and chaotic society.

As he pondered, she now began to shift and stir from her sleep. Reaching her arms above her head in a blind stretch and arching her back, she let out a cute little noise from her lips. It was the noise she made every morning before she opened her eyes, a noise that always made him smile.

Finally her black eyelashes fluttered open, revealing icy blue eyes from behind her sleepy lids. They were bright and beautiful, especially in the early morning sunlight.

"Good morning." She smiled warmly as she rolled over on her side to face him, tossing her long locks onto one side of her head and using them as a makeshift pillow beneath her left cheek as she looked up at him. She yawned and blinked a few times to clear the sleep from her eyes.

He stroked her hair that fell on the pillow, liquid gold forming small waves and pools on the red satin beneath. "Good morning, Celeste." His own eyes stayed on her hair as he played with it between his fingertips. Even after their late night adventures, her hair still smelled wonderful, as did her skin as he leaned down to kiss her shoulder and gently nibble on it.

She giggled her wonderful, tinkling laughter and ran her fingertips through his aging hair. She playfully pulled it back in a sharp tug that made him gasp as he was forced to lean up from her. *Another red flag,* he thought to himself. *This girl is trouble,* he admitted to himself as he straddled on top of her, but didn't care as he leaned down to seal her mouth with his.

She embraced her newfound position beneath him, raising her hips to feel his hard morning cock glide against her, warm and stiff. He ran two fingers against the entrance between her legs and felt the warm heat welcome him as she softly inhaled into his kiss. She was already wet and waiting for him to enter, but that wouldn't be the plan for today as his phone at the bedside chirped.

It had occurred so often since they had met over a year ago that it didn't disappoint her anymore, not that she would ever admit it if it did—a good submissive would never admit to such a thing. However, she wasn't just a submissive now, was she? Knowing how to read people, he acknowledged her reactions, and it indeed used to bother her. Another red flag.

Chapter Two

The phone call he received at his bedside indicated there was a body at one of the more popular areas for crime on the east side of the city. No more, no less. That's why they called him and his partner, because that was all there was to tell at that time. It was up to him and Detective Bob Donahue to decipher the rest.

He walked past the boys in uniform and ducked beneath the yellow crime tape. As usual, one of the young cops held it up for him. They knew who he was by now and offered a small nod of a greeting as he arrived on scene. He was highly respected in his field, and part of it came from the lineage of his name and family tree in the department.

He knew that in a culture so engulfed in pleasure and instant gratification, it was rare for someone to want to examine the darker side of life. Not the darkness offered by fantasy and roleplaying, but the real darkness. The darkness that, if you let it in it, could swallow anything good about you and leave an empty shell of a human in its wake.

Yet, while this was the job he didn't exactly choose, it was the job he was born into and made the best of. Ironically enough, it was a good fit, as he didn't think there was much left for that darkness to claim after all he had seen since he was an adolescent; and not to brag, but maybe that was what made him so good at his job.

The morning hours had already burned away, as had the initial jolt of caffeine from the coffee he'd drunk on the way from his apartment to this side of town. He was surprised the coffee helped at all—he'd drunk so much of it over the years that he had developed a pretty high tolerance for the caffeinated beverage. However, the sight of the body in the distance began to release a new type of adrenaline into his blood, and he'd be firing off of those cylinders soon.

His partner had already arrived on the scene, and from his facial expression as he looked up to greet Ellis from the sight of the deceased body, it appeared he had been there for quite a while. *Mr. Punctuality,* Ellis thought to himself, returning his morning greeting.

Donahue was a good man, with more years on the force than he himself had already accumulated. They had been working together for three years now, and while they weren't exactly buddies, there were some things you get to know about someone when you work with them day in and day out for that long. Especially on a job like this.

For instance, he knew Donahue was involved in a monogamous relationship with a fellow rope enthusiast like himself. This was the type of interest that allows you to have a home with a white picket fence and two children; and that's exactly what Donahue had. In fact, now he had a third on the way.

Ellis wasn't sure how his partner could take seeing this brutality day in and day out. Being the father of soon-to-be three children, he knew it would personally screw him up. Christ, one of Donahue's kids was a girl not too far away from her tenth birthday, when her training would begin. If she identified as a submissive, which Donahue had indicated he assumed in their past conversations she was going to be, how could this job still not affect him?

How would he be able to look at all of the chewed-up bodies they pulled out of the rivers, or the mutilated body dumps they recovered from burned and charred car trunks or in alley dumpsters? So many of them were young, submissive girls.

He gave him an abundant amount of credit for sticking with the job for so many years, but he could tell it would soon be quitting time. A man could only take so much of this lifestyle on the force. Detecting was a young man's game, but with the shortage of good detectives on the scene, it urged many of them to stay on as long as they could bear it. The pay wasn't half bad either. However, looking down into his partner's face, now he could see the years of working crime scene after crime scene had indeed taken its toll.

"What do we have here?" he asked, bending down to be eye-to-eye with his partner to oversee the details of their victim.

"Looks like a body dump. I'm betting she was killed somewhere else and dropped off here sometime in the early morning before the rain." He moved her arm, which was wet from the new rainfall, to reveal the dry patch of pavement underneath.

"Well, there goes our evidence." Ellis muttered.

Moving his eyes over the victim, he wasn't surprised Donahue thought she'd been dumped there. It wasn't uncommon for bodies to pop up on this side of town, it was where the lower tertiary tier of kinksters lived, and was an area all too familiar with all types of crime. This was also where traveling pop-up clubs appeared, instead of safe, clean, and monitored brick-and-mortar dungeons with good reputations.

The area homed a vast array of abandoned warehouses where clubs could easily be set up, played hard in for a night or two, then abandoned once again. In two or three weeks, another one would pop up and start the cycle all over again. They regularly moved from building to building, because where there were unsafe kink practices, there were also usually other forms of illegal activity.

The girl they were there to collect couldn't have been more than nineteen or twenty years old, but Ellis had been proven wrong before. Once on the autopsy table, stripped of clothes, hosed down, and scrubbed clean of makeup by the medical examiner, one girl who may have looked twenty-one coming in could easily appear to be thirty-five going out.

However, makeup and clothes weren't the only factors that could be misleading when trying to figure out an identity, and it only became worse as you moved up in the sectors of society. Once money was involved—real money—plastic surgery and Botox were easily obtainable, and almost as addicting as the fetish-filled lifestyles the patients lived.

The only good thing that came out of elective body modification, whether it be breast implants, buttock implants, or an array of other costly procedures, was the serial number that was placed under the skin with each modification. These numbers were extremely useful and had helped greatly in identifying vics in past cases.

Unfortunately, when the less privileged received body modification, their pieces usually didn't come through the reputable and legal channels of the higher class. No serial numbers, no medical records. Hell, half the time it wasn't even a real doctor performing the operation!

A desperate soul, a folding table, and a local anesthetic in the form of 100% grain alcohol was all some could afford. However, you can't pick and choose what gets you off in this world, and if anyone knew that, it was Ellis.

If being transformed into a bimbo-bot with size DDD breasts and pillow lips did it for you, then you would find a way to become this idea of beauty. If being a cat-boy with clipped ears and filed fangs for teeth fueled your pecker, then there was always someone willing to take your money and make it happen.

Looking down on this poor girl now, he moved on from estimating her age and looked at the more concrete facts. She was short, maybe five foot two, yet it was hard to tell since she was lying in such an awkward and unnatural position. Her neck was arched into her chest, and both of her legs were bent in at the knees so her feet rested right under her bum as she lay on her side. It appeared to be a very odd fetal position.

One glittered platform heel remained on her foot, while the other was apparently lost to the events which had resulted in her being left here. Her clothes were black vinyl—a short skirt and matching bra. Basic club wear for kids. The slick fabric had collected some of the raindrops from the storm earlier that morning, but most had rolled off, given the nature of vinyl, and had undoubtedly washed away any evidence with it.

Her body was frail, almost sickly so. *Oh, what people did to themselves to reach their desired goal of what they found attractive?* While this fell short of body modification, you could easily see the victim's spine beneath the skin along her back as she was curled into that oddly suggestive bent position. Her arms, which were tucked into herself, revealed small, delicate wrists, but there were no track marks mapped out along the inside. *Not a junkie.*

Drugs were rare in this world, even here in the bad part of town, but if you *were* to find them, they were usually involved with pop-up clubs, where they were used to enhance experiences. However, they weren't like the drugs of the past. They were far less addicting, and were more like mood enhancers.

While the old-world narcotics were still available if you knew where to look and who to ask, an adrenaline-filled kink experience had replaced the urge to use drugs a long time ago. However, left in their place was a new opportunity for dangerous and addicting behavior, and that was the means in which these BDSM scenarios were conducted. In fact, some were in many ways more dangerous than drugs themselves had ever been, and that is why cops wanted to crack down on these elusive pop-up clubs and unsafe practices.

Blood- and fluid-transmitted diseases were at a record high since this lifestyle had taken root in every man, woman and young adult's life. Not to mention, the scenes they acted out could snuff out a life in a hot minute if something went wrong. Knife play, breath play … even rope bondage could asphyxiate or permanently injure nerves and induce paralysis. In this lifestyle, the scenes exhibited ran the gamut from light and fluffy to extremely hardcore and dangerous.

Ellis looked closer at the girl's neck and saw this may have been the case here, as he could see bruise marks. He felt his cock begin to harden at the sight, so he shifted his position. Donahue's gaze remained on the corpse, not noticing his partner's unease.

That same thought from before ran across his mind again—*you can't help what turns you on*—and, in this case, asphyxiation was one of the detective's weak points by being his preferred fetish amongst an extensive list of interests. He pushed it out of his mind—his sense of self-control was a skill he valued as a detective, and he was easily able to return to the matter at hand… *but sometimes you just can't help where your mind momentarily takes you.*

He examined the side of her neck closely, this time from a purely investigative standpoint. It looked like finger bruises, but the M.E. would know for sure.

Donahue got to his feet with a groan, his age showing after being crouched down so long. "No collar," he mentioned as he followed his partner's eyeline to the victim's neck. "I'm going to go see if any of the boys in blue saw it. Maybe it came off during the struggle and one of them bagged it up as evidence."

Doubtful, Ellis thought to himself, but nodded in agreement to his partner before Donahue stalked away toward the yellow tape.

Ellis walked around the body and lowered himself back down to the ground, his erection still hard and at attention. He hunkered down by the girl to get a better look. With a latex-gloved hand he pressed two fingers against her hairline, moving her pink wig back an inch or two to reveal a wig cap. A lock of brunette hair escaped from beneath the wet pink artificial hair, revealing her true color.

Was anything about this girl real? he wondered.

As the morning sun rose in the sky, sunbeams peeked out from behind the clouds and over the building. The natural morning light made him notice something he hadn't before. Her eyelids sparkled unnaturally. However, this wasn't from glitter like club kids usually wore—this sparkle wasn't synthetic. It was something he thought he had seen before, but would need to have confirmed by the M.E. to be sure.

He removed a plastic test tube from the inside of his coat pocket and took out the long swab cradled inside. Usually these were reserved for DNA cheek swabs, and, while not the intended use, it would work just fine.

He gently glided the cotton tip along one eyelid, lifting some of the bluish-green iridescent pigment from her skin. He placed it back into the tube, sealing it with a click. He was lucky the rain hadn't dissolved this evidence.

"No dice," his partner announced as he returned to the scene from his collar-hunting expedition. He then saw the freshly collected makeup in Ellis's hand. "What do you think it is?"

"The lab will tell us for sure," he answered without meeting his gaze, placing the container safely back inside the pocket of his coat.

He could start to hear the squawk and chatter of the early morning lookie-loos on their way to work. Mixed in with their voices was the press who'd gathered at the yellow crime scene tape behind them. He was surprised he hadn't had to battle them on his way in; news usually traveled fast around these parts. Regardless, they were here now, and the natives were becoming restless as they demanded answers from the police who stood guard at the crime scene entrance. It was time to make their exit and let the local law enforcement do their job.

Chapter Three

While the coroner's floor was a frequent stop for Ellis during his investigations, he could never get used to the smell. Nor did he particularly enjoy the sound of an electric bone saw slicing through skullcaps, which he had heard on more than one occasion to his visits to the basement. It was like a dentist drill going through a tooth, only amplified by ten. Fortunately, as he made his way down the corridor today, he didn't hear anyone revving up and getting ready to grind.

Yet the smell was still there. It was *always* there, heavy and thick. He would have to go home and shower, but not even the strongest exfoliator could purge that scent from his memory.

When he'd asked at the directory where his body from this morning had been sent, he knew the medical examiner assigned to his case. Doctor Jensen. He was a finicky old fart who had been cutting up bodies since long before Ellis was on the force, probably even before Donahue was a detective.

Nothing phased him, and if you didn't see his work through his well-experienced and opinionated lens, then you and he were not going to get along. Suffice it to say, he wasn't the most pleasant man to work with. However, as much as it pained Ellis to admit, he was still one of the best medical examiners the city had to offer. In a city of pleasure, who would want to cut up bodies for a living?

The detective stopped before he entered the third examination room on the left. The name card below the door number read "Jensen, Frank, M.E." Great. He took one last breath of the tainted, foul smelling air, because he knew once he stepped inside, his nose would be assaulted full-on by the scent of formaldehyde and embalming fluid. The odor he was experiencing now in the hallway was simply an amuse-bouche to the main course awaiting inside.

No turning back now.

Once inside, it hit him like a tidal wave. He tried to maintain his composure, but the M.E. saw it right away as he looked up from his paperwork at his desk across from the door. A pleased, almost sadistic smile spread across his dry, aged lips. Yet instead of responding with a quick-witted comment or a jab to verbally rib the seasoned detective, as was the history between Ellis and Doc. Jensen, all he said tonight was, "Good evening, Detective."

Ellis offered a stern nod. "Evening, Jensen." He exhaled the sentence and immediately tasted the odor of chemicals that filled his nostrils, now laying thickly on his tongue and making its way to the back of his throat. He feigned a cough into his fist to try and clear it. No luck.

Now that the pleasantries were out of the way, they could get down to business. While he wasn't a fan of the old man, he was glad he didn't have to lengthen his stay in the basement by bullshitting and making small talk that never amounted to anything.

Ellis wasn't the type to make small talk with anyone, except maybe Donahue or Celeste. However, even when in her company, they were usually too busy with each other to let things like conversation get in the way of their good time. It wasn't unless he took her to dinner or an event that the two exchanged stories and idle chitchat, and even though Ellis would never admit it to anyone else, he actually enjoyed it with her.

While Jensen was not one for small talk himself, the old man *did* love to talk about the dead: causes of death, decomposition rate, rigor mortis, the embalming process. From the way he talked about it, Ellis wondered if the doc had a closeted necrophilia fetish. Despite his distaste not only for the coroner but also the profession itself, Ellis had to hand it to the guy—he knew his shit.

With what appeared to be a jaunt in his step, a walk only a man who loved his work could display, Jensen made his way over to the body covered by a sheet on one of the three exam tables. He was like Willy Wonka—with the dead bodies, vials of specimens, and foul smelling chemicals all the pride and joy of his beloved chocolate factory.

Pulling the cloth back from the body without any warning, Ellis could barely tell it was the same vic as the woman he had examined this morning in the alley. The body before him looked more like a woman in her late twenties than the young adult that had been laid before him in the street. With the black vinyl gone, makeup removed, and that horrible pink wig hopefully tossed into the garbage or burned, the woman before him looked like anything but a club kid. *Duped again, old boy*, he thought to himself.

As she was stretched out now on the cold metal table before him, he newly estimated her height to be in the neighborhood of five foot four, maybe. He understood why she was wearing the high heels. She no longer rested in that strange fetal position which he had found her in earlier, and in a natural resting position on her back she appeared to weigh even less than he initially assumed.

Besides the "Y" incision from the coroner's examination of her internal organs, the marks on her body weren't life threatening at all. Sure, there were lots of bumps and bruises that covered her now sickly-pale skin. Some were fresh, and she had probably sustained them shortly before her demise, but others were in various stages of healing from a few days or even a week ago. However, none had broken the skin. As far as he could tell, none were in direct relation to what had taken this woman's life.

"Another bottom bunny," the doc muttered.

This was a term used for bottoms who participated in light bondage play, but rarely engaged in any behaviors that would leave more than a bruise, and certainly nothing long lasting such as scars or other permanent marks.

A bunny's main purpose in life was to serve and be beautiful. A concubine. They were to be companions to their Owners, and occasionally take a beating that made real pain aficionados in attendance roll their eyes, as it was obvious the doc was doing now.

"No scars, no tattoos, no identifying marks of any kind. Nothing except this." He took her right palm and turned it over. In the soft flesh of her open hand, a single gash extended from the base of her middle finger down to the heel of her palm. "It was made post mortem," he explained. "As far as an identity, if she's been tested, we'll find her in the blood bank records."

In a world where practicing kink, polyamory, and casual sex was as common as watching prime time television in the 1990s, everyone had been tested at least one time or another in their life—or so you would hope, when you were in the midst of a sexual tryst with someone new.

Despite how normalized casual sex was in their culture, it was still an awkward conversation to have when you were out of condoms and decided to forgo the risk and ride bareback.

A five-minute appointment every six months at a local center was the recommendation for everyone, from the highest ranks in society to the lowest. All insurances covered this, but it was those on the bottom that would commonly avoid the process altogether. It wasn't cheap to pay out-of-pocket, and to be out of a job and tested twice a year added up to big expenses.

As for the primary class, they had their own private clinics and doctors who visited their lavish estates and mansions. He had even heard rumors of no one being allowed to work the grounds or attend parties without an up-to-date documentation showing their clean bill of health from the past month.

There were even whispers about a new technology that would place a chip beneath your wrist upon birth that would glow different colors when an STD was detected. If you had more than one, then the colors would alternate. Soon there would be no hiding. Until that day came, there was the old-fashioned way of pricks and pokes to obtain a blood sample. As much as things had changed, they had also stayed the same.

Sure, there were other alternatives. Stores sold paper strips that tested for the main STDs: HIV, chlamydia, and herpes. All it would take was drop of blood on the paper, and it would turn black or green to indicate the presence of an STD. It was similar to how the old pregnancy tests worked—one line for an empty oven, two lines and you're a winner … so to speak. While inexpensive and a conveniently fast alternative, the problem with these paper strips was that they weren't always accurate. Ellis had heard of many false positives, and even more false negatives.

There was also a mail kit that cost a fraction of the cost of a full panel work-up at the clinic, but this came with its own problems. You would have to send in your own blood sample that would need to be drawn yourself, using a kit you sent away for. You could never be sure whether they wouldn't mix up or accidentally cross-contaminate your blood with someone else's, and if that wasn't bad enough, it took weeks or even a month to get your results. Some people didn't get their results back at all! With the inaccuracies, waiting times, and scams, Ellis could see why those who couldn't afford the clinic's routine testing threw caution to the wind—and that is exactly what many did.

Diseases ran rampant amongst the lower faction, and with the addiction of kink being what it was in their society, people would still play and fuck despite the consequences. Many would rather take the instant gratification of a good time and deal with the consequences later. This was called "kink roulette."

"We'll know what her blood says in the morning," Doc Jensen said, as if reading the detective's mind.

"Is there anything you *do* know?" he groaned, rubbing his hand through his aging hair. He was becoming restless with fatigue, and the smell of formaldehyde was making him dizzy.

"Of course," the doctor rebuffed, obviously insulted. "The cause of death." Standing at the head of the metal table, he placed two gloved hands beneath the victim's jaw line and pulled her head back, brushing away the stray strands of hazelnut hair that rested along her neck and shoulders. He exposed the soft, supple skin of her neck in the bright fluorescent light overhead.

"Strangulation. Quick and easy." He paused for a moment considering his statement. "Well, maybe not *quick.*"

Ellis leaned down and observed the markings.

"It takes someone with a considerable amount of muscle to choke our girl here with enough strength, or hatred, to break the hyoid bone. In fact, not just strength, but time. Do you see her eyes?"

The medical examiner opened the woman's eyelids with his gloved hand to expose her glassy, dead stare up at the ceiling. The once-white sclera was now flooded with blood.

"Petechial hemorrhaging in the eyes, a main indicator of asphyxiation. The blood vessels were popped in both eyes, as the brain was deprived of oxygen for a prolonged period of time. While our girl here didn't put up much of a fight, it probably still took around two or three minutes of continuous pressure before the perp let her go." He released her eyelids so she appeared to just be sleeping again. Crossing his arms superiorly over his chest, he continued. "Do you know how brutal three minutes of continuous strangulation can be? What it *feels* like? Christ, each second must have felt like an eternity after the initial fifteen seconds. If she was lucky, she passed out before death finally came for her."

"I have a vague idea what that feels like," Ellis said dryly, trying to hide his excitement at the mere mention of the type of fetish that made his blood boil. He could feel his heart pound against the inside of his chest. God, he hoped the doc didn't notice. In the silence of the M.E.'s room, he could practically hear it.

If the doctor did make the connection, he paid him no mind as he continued his speech, which oddly felt a little rehearsed to the detective as he listened.

"He may have even hung on for an extra minute or two before he was absolutely certain she was dead. In which time"—he snapped the latex glove off of his hand, startling Ellis as he stood up from the body—"he undoubtedly felt the breaking of the hyoid pop beneath his fingers."

Ellis shot him a glare but the doc didn't notice; he was too far into his moment of self-indulgence as he continued his medical mumbo-jumbo.

"You can see how deep the bruising is, indicating how hard the pressure he used had to have been." He indicated along the neckline right below the chin where two deep, dark impressions lay symmetrically placed. "No doubt, the thumb marks."

He lifted up the hair to expose the far sides of her neck where four other bruises burrowed into her skin on each side.

"However, the multiple sets of finger bruises along the neck here and here indicate he choked her repeatedly. Either he didn't have a firm grip, or, more likely the case, our perp choked her, then let her go to breathe, and then choked her again." He demonstrated with his hands. "Never did he remove his thumbs as he straddled over her. He had to maintain a constant presence of power and control. That's why those bruises are so deep."

That was something Ellis could relate to all too well. As a Dominant, you had to impose your mental and physical strength over your submissive so they knew who was fully in charge. You could not give them a choice. Now looking at this woman, Ellis knew she that not only had she not had a choice, she'd never even had a hope.

"Looking at these bruises on the side of her neck," the doctor continued, "I'm assuming he strangled and revived her at least half a dozen times before finally finishing the job, no doubt watching her eyes each time she faded out to the brink of unconsciousness and came back to awareness. It must have been terrifying."

Hearing all of this talk of straddling, asphyxia, and having full control over someone, Ellis's cock betrayed him as it had earlier that morning. He tried to remain on point.

"Any prints?"

The doctor glared at the detective over the top of his glasses, as if scolding him for asking such an obviously dumb question. "No, they wore gloves."

The detective shrugged. "Figured it was worth asking."

"Not only were there no prints, before you ask any more moronic questions," the doctor scoffed for emphasis, "the body was also clean of any hairs, fluids, and fibers."

While the old man hadn't got his jabs off when Ellis had first entered his office, he sure was coming into the ring punching and swinging away now.

Ellis took the verbal jabs; these were questions he had to ask. "Could it have been a scene gone wrong?"

The doctor resumed that same look of irritation on his face that only Ellis could bring out in him. "Aren't *you* supposed to tell *me* that, Detective?"

"Humor me, Doc." This was the point where Ellis would usually stern up his own tone, but he was in no mood to banter—not tonight; he was too tired.

"Sure, especially given where you found her. Adrenaline junkies are always pushing the limit to get closer and closer to that unobtainable first high. In fact, I think our girl here was an asphyxiation enthusiast at one time or another, from the coloration of the skin along her neck."

Now something inside of Ellis stirred excitedly, more so than the blood pumping to his nearly-erect penis. He pushed it as far down as he could, but it was being more and more difficult to control. It was a hunger he didn't want to acknowledge, but one that overtook him—a tingle in the back of his mind that was connected to a memory, but it was a memory he was determined to keep locked away there.

"It looks like she resorted to self-strangulation, see how the flesh has a slight grey hue to it? No doubt she covered it with makeup on a daily basis. The skin sometimes takes on a gooseflesh quality as well, for those who indulge in self-strangulation on a regular basis. However, hers doesn't seem to have done so. Maybe she was just a beginner."

Seeing the girl laid out like this, he noticed something he hadn't been able to observe at the crime scene, given the unusual position of her body. Her waist appeared smaller than her frame would allow, even when taking into consideration how tiny she was to begin with.

"Is she emaciated?"

He followed the detective's eyes to her waist. "No. She was waist training, and to get results this good, she was most likely using a steel-boned corset. Many women who have passed their prime resort to this method to obtain that smaller frame they once had in their spring-chicken days."

"Those aren't cheap," he muttered, more to himself than to the doc, and then he looked up at him. "Was this girl from the tertiary sector?"

"Not necessarily. The body, the way she took care of herself, her presentation—all lead me to believe you might have a vic from the middle. I've seen tertiaries come in here who have attempted waist training before. They'd resort to duct tape or rope, but, as you can see, there are no irritation marks or rope burns from the repeated bindings with such primitive means." He thought for a moment. "It's possible she purchased the corset on the market."

"Even on the market, they're not cheap—that's a pretty hard expense to swallow."

The old man looked up to him, raising an eyebrow in indication of a joke that was just behind his lips, on the tip of his tongue, but the twinkle in his eye said it all. It made Ellis's stomach turn, even though he was the biggest hypocrite in the world for saying so, as his cock was now rock hard and swollen, throbbing beneath his slacks.

They never discussed each other's kinks, a common topic amongst anyone in the culture, and this was one kink that Ellis had neither reason nor need to divulge to this man. Ever.

Seeing the detective wasn't going to take the bait, Jensen turned on his heel and walked disappointedly back to his desk. "I'll have more information for you in the morning when the results come back," he told the detective flatly, returning to his paperwork.

Ellis gratefully began to make his way for the door when something popped into his mind and he suddenly stopped to turn back. "Oh, that swab I sent over…"

"Oh, yes." The old man fussed with some items on his desk and held up the tube that contained the swab Ellis had collected earlier that day. "Well, your suspicions were correct about one thing. The substance on her eyelids was not a synthetic makeup at all. It was—"

"Blue Morpho pigments," the detective finished for him.

"Yeah, how did you know?"

"The top tier uses carefully collected and crushed pigments from the Blue Morpho butterflies for their eyes instead of makeup. It's a status thing."

"Actually, it's not the wings that are crushed up to achieve the 'dust' they use for their eyelids." Oh, how he enjoyed correcting Ellis. "The powder on their wings is actually tiny scales from small modified hairs on the butterfly's wings. They are carefully collected along the forewings and hind wings. Once the butterflies are stripped of their beauty, they are disposed of." He nodded in the direction of the exam table where their Jane Doe rested. "Apparently, much like our girl here."

Ellis let the old man have his moment of wisdom before he responded. "I get it. It's hard to come by. So how the hell did she get her hands on it?" he wondered to himself, rather than imposing the question to the doctor. "Not only is it expensive, it's highly coveted and unobtainable by anyone in the bottom two tiers, unless of course you know someone and are willing to pay an arm and a leg."

A moment of silence passed between them.

"Then perhaps you're looking for your killer in the primary tier, Detective." The old man suggested with a grin that revealed he was jesting. No one in the primary tier would ever commit such a heinous act. Even though the doc had meant it as a joke, Ellis hoped he was wrong. Dead wrong.

Chapter Four

Entering into his apartment, he threw his overcoat and suit jacket onto the couch. He could still detect the sweet scent of Celeste in his home, but there was something else ... oh yes, toy cleaner. No doubt she had cleaned the toys they had used the prior night and placed them back in their proper places. This was something she always did before leaving his apartment, whether he was home to see her off or not. She was such a good girl.

Walking into his bedroom and opening his walk-in closet, he saw this was indeed the case. This is where he kept his collection of toys displayed proudly, and she knew where each and every one of them belonged. Closing the door to his collection, he even saw she had made the bed before she let herself out. He expected no less, but it still pleased him to see it today as much as it had pleased him the first time.

As was her usual M.O., a piece of paper was folded once over and placed on his pillow. His name was scrawled on it, in her fancy handwriting that complemented her high-class personality. How she managed to make three little letters look so beautiful was beyond him.

He sat at the foot of his bed and unfolded the paper.

Wes,

As always, it was such an honor as well as a pleasure to serve you last night. Your caring eyes as you caressed my hair before you allowed me to suffer beneath you at your hands speaks volumes, and I hope we can continue our journey together soon.

Always

~ c

With a small smile and a tinge of emptiness, for lack of a better word, he opened his beside drawer and added the note to the others he had collected from her over the months. Her perfume wafted out from the drawer of papers; no doubt each of them had gently been sprayed with the sweet scent she commonly wore. He had to hand it to her, the girl had skills, and she knew how to invest in repeat customers.

***

After Ellis had taken a long, hot shower, he thankfully had the scent of Celeste's perfume still resonating on his pillowcase and bed sheets to replace the putrid stench of the coroner's office, even if the scent of chemicals was in fact just in his memory at this point.

He palmed his cock beneath the blanket; it was already half hard. In just a few meaningful strokes, he felt himself instantly respond and grow thick and solid within his hand.

Ellis could feel the stress of the day begin to fade away as his hand worked effortlessly up and down his shaft. He smoothly pulled and released the foreskin up and down over the pink head of his cock, feeling himself begin to throb with excitement against his palm.

Not even a full twenty-four hours had passed since he had last touched Celeste's lips to his, but he still craved them fiercely. He recalled when his tongue had danced across hers, and then graced the soft delicate skin of her neck. The way she'd let out her little sighs when he'd bitten into the delicate spot where her neck met her shoulder resonated in his ears. His cock tightened in his hand at the mere thought of how smooth her breasts had felt beneath his hands.

He remembered how he had made her moan and sigh with pleasure, and then cry out in pain. How those wonderful sounds had mixed together in a symphony he'd composed at his own hands, sounds that he could replicate with her again and again because he knew so many ways to bring her pleasure, and even more ways to bring her pain. It was music that still rang in his ears as he stroked himself faster.

His mind's eye focused on how her red painted lips wrapped around his cock, and that innocent look she gave him when she looked up from working him in and out of her mouth. Those big blue eyes, bright and sweet. His lovely blue-eyed girl.

She would wrap her warm mouth around his cock and, as she danced her skilled tongue along him, she would take him deeper, first examining the delicate pink head with the tip of her tongue, and then lapping her tongue fully against it, warm and wet. Her hand tightly held his shaft and worked him up and down.

She would then move her hand down toward the base and slide him along her tongue until he felt himself push into the entrance of her soft throat. She was so hot, so wet and soft. The sound of her sucking harder and faster in his memory matched his own movements as he felt himself inching toward that inevitable climax.

He closed his eyes, thinking of how, just hours ago, he'd shot his cum deep inside of her. As she had him fully in her throat and her face was buried against him, she'd sucked and lapped and stroked her tongue against his shaft, working his cum up, and then he felt himself let go and erupt in thick streams. He kept pumping his cock to Celeste's memory as he felt his cum spread out across his stomach beneath the bed sheets.

He squeezed the last drops from the head of his spent cock, her ethereal image still lingering behind his closed eyelids, her perfume still filling his nostrils as he closed his eyes for the night.

Chapter Five

Celeste's Story

It hadn't been that long ago when he'd first met his blue-eyed girl, but the connection they had made was instantaneous. From the moment he'd noticed she was watching him across the bar, he had been intrigued, and when he approached her, she must have been confident she had him right then and there—hook, line, and sinker. Looking back on it now, that was probably why her blue eyes danced with intensity, a sense of power which he couldn't recognize at the time.

He sauntered over to where she was sitting alone at an empty table in a bar full of patrons. She was the definition of bait—young, beautiful, vulnerable. It couldn't have been more obvious if she had been sitting on the metal plate of a bear trap. Yet he found himself being drawn into her. *Who had the real power here?*

She had a long-stemmed wine glass between her delicately thin fingers as he approached. With a wave of her free hand, she offered him a seat in the empty chair. The gesture was accompanied by a small, close-lipped smile and a subtle raise of an eyebrow that would make anyone, man or woman, follow her silent gesture to be seated. No, not gesture—her wordless command. In retrospect he could see that now, and her silent act of power made him hot for her all the more.

He remembered that night as if it was yesterday, right down to what she was wearing and the way she smelled. It wasn't just her perfume that had wafted to his nose and struck his brain. There was an underlying scent that he would come to know, because as her perfume, lotions, and grooming products changed, that same underlying scent was still there. It was her scent, and it made his mouth water. It was unique to her and triggered his sex drive, tempting him to take her instantaneously, right then and there on the bar table that fateful evening. It had taken all of his restraint not to.

He'd soon learned her taste was just as powerful. The first night they met was also the first night their lips touched, and the taste that danced upon her tongue and traveled along his taste buds was just as tantalizing as her scent, yet amplified tenfold, and it wasn't just her tongue. The skin along her neck, her shoulders, her breasts, everywhere he traced his tongue along her body held that same alluring and delicious flavor.

From that first conversation, there was something that sparked between them which they both felt equally and strong, and since then, they were inseparable when they reunited each and every time thereafter.

Their interests inside the bedroom complemented each other, almost to a fault. While they had plenty of mutual interests outside of fetish, kink, and sex, they rarely did anything else when they were together, especially the first six months.

They discovered, much to their shared amusement, that self-control was not their strong suit. Words were rarely exchanged as she arrived at his apartment. Clothes weren't even removed half of the time before he had taken her. This wasn't restricted to his apartment, but to shared moments in public as well. Club bathrooms, abandoned alleys, his car— all of it was fair game.

Their bond of hedonism and pleasure fed one another, and as insatiable as each were to their other partners, their sessions would always leave them worn and exhausted by the time they parted ways. They soon discovered their longing for each other and their insatiable appetite for one another would only increase the longer they were apart.

Their attraction and passion for each other was like nothing he had ever felt, and he could tell watching her blue eyes beg for him in every way imaginable that she felt the same, even if she never let it cross her perfect lips.

Ellis would drag her to the bedroom by a handful of her golden locks and throw her down onto the bed, where she would quickly right herself in time for his advances. If he didn't like her in that position, he would silently let her know as he grabbed her arms and legs and adjusted her to how he wished.

The energy between them was explosive at best and volatile at worst, involving bruised ribs, teeth marks that broke through the skin, and an occasional busted lip. However, all of it was consensual, and even when accidents happened, their play continued, intense and fierce.

Neither of them had regrets, even when they awoke the next morning mutually sore, and she often deeply bruised. They were like two animals, savage and wild, and each of them was the other's personal playground.

When they ventured out into public, she was a proper lady, capturing the eyes of both men and women they passed on the street or sat alongside in restaurants. She could easily make conversation about any topic, from pop culture to classical music and even politics outside of their region. Many times he just sat and watched how people responded to her, how they stared and desired her company for themselves. Ellis wasn't a fool; he was proud to have her on his arm, and damned lucky to have her in his bed.

Those first six months were a whirlwind, but as their time together continued, he didn't see her as often as he would have liked. Work would get in the way for him, dates and other suitors would take up time for her, but whenever they reconnected, so did their passion and uncanny and endless energy for the other.

***

Celeste wasn't a traditional bottom in any sense of the word; she was feisty, unpredictable, and could take pain better than anyone he had ever played with before. When they were together, he didn't have to hold back, because of her high tolerance for pain and open-mindedness to try almost anything, and that was a first.

In fact, on more than one occasion he'd felt he had to hold back because of *his* own boundaries. This was something that was rare for any Dominant to experience. Most often the bottom's boundaries would be approached before the Top's, and this excited him in a way that he could not put his finger on.

No one had ever pushed him physically or mentally before, and it was an extremely foreign feeling to the seasoned and well-experienced Dom. The challenge of being with her was intoxicating, and it was like a drug that kept him hooked and coming back to her for more. In return, he wondered why she returned to him. What was her allure, and why had she continued seeing him since their initial meeting in the bar? This was something that plagued his thoughts, especially in the beginning. Surely she could do better.

He knew it wasn't love, and, while lust had a large part to do with it, he wondered what else it could be. Finally, one night when she was curled up next to him in his bed which they had stripped from its covers, blankets, and pillows, she had told him. It was because he made her feel safe, and she knew no matter what they did and what her body endured, he would never truly hurt her.

Chapter Six

The next morning, with the thoughts of Celeste fading with the morning fog, Ellis and Donahue hit the streets to try and find out more information in regards to their homicide victim. The medical examiner had sent them images to assist them on their routine follow-up, and they finally had a name—Yvonne Walters.

Doc Jensen had also sent them a picture documenting what he had found as he followed up on a hunch. When he'd run a black light over Yvonne's body, the indigo glow of the hot light revealed a hidden tattoo on the back of her right hand. It was the size of a quarter and contained the image of two riding crops making an "X." It was an intricate amount of detail for such a small tattoo. The detectives assumed it was most likely a tattoo that allowed access into the underground clubs, much like the one where she had met her demise the night before.

The symbol itself wasn't familiar to either of the men, but it was to the medical examiner. He'd told Ellis he had come across it on quite a few John and Jane Does over the past couple of years.

While the particular image itself was not familiar, the use of a hidden tattoo only to be revealed by black light was not a new concept to anyone on the force, or in the lifestyle. It was a common method for entrance into clubs. In exchange for receiving the tattoo, the club goer would pay monthly dues. If they couldn't afford the cash, payment would commonly be taken in other forms, mostly sex or indulging in a club organizer's particular fetish.

Taking one of their nondescript undercover cars was surely the way to go in the tertiary tier of the area. Both detectives owned cars that were far from inconspicuous, so they were able to borrow one from the undercover unit. Now at least they'd have a car to actually return to.

The way the tertiary tier looked, right down to the way it smelled, was downright repugnant in this area of town. It was somewhere along the crossroads of cheap alcohol, day-old vomit rotting in the sun, and fresh urine. The men soon found out that depending on which street you traveled, the dominant scent amongst the three would change, but never would the putrid stench dissipate completely.

Unlike the scent in the morgue, you did tend to get used to this unique aroma. That is, until a breeze stirred up something extra nasty and wafted it right under your nose. Yet if you stayed downtown long enough, and today it appeared they certainly would be, it wasn't beyond the realm of possibility to get used to it. From the looks of it, it was going to be a very, very long day.

Starting with the area where the body was initially found, the two detectives asked local store owners if their surveillance cameras had caught anything.

To neither of the detectives' surprise, they received a mixture of responses ranging from "they don't work," to "they're dummy cams," and, finally, the most popular response of all—"What cameras?" followed by mocking laughter.

The lower class was indeed destitute. Iron bars on business windows, accompanied by a shotgun behind the counter, was a more reasonable investment than an alarm system that police would never respond to. Security cameras ran the chance of malfunctioning, or more likely getting shot out as soon as the perps came into the establishment.

The tertiary tier policed their own, and Ellis didn't blame them. He knew how unlikely cops were to patrol these streets at night. It was a gamble that not many wanted to take. Many of these young men and women had families they wanted to return to at the end of their work shift, and this part of town was extremely unpredictable and their safety wasn't guaranteed.

In time, the people who lived here learned they couldn't count on the cops, so they took justice into their own hands, in their businesses as well as their homes and in the streets. Vigilante justice wasn't uncommon here.

The cops weren't just distrusted; it was no secret they were downright despised by most in this part of town, and this made their unwelcomed visit dangerous. With their nice suites, closely clipped haircuts, and solemn demeanors, they were easily pegged as law enforcement as soon as they hit the streets.

Now, as they showed the picture of their victim around to shop owners as well as people on the street, the responses they received were no better. And when asked about the club location from the night before, they all played dumb.

Ellis could tell from observing the body language of those he questioned that many of them knew much more than they were willing to divulge.

***

The detectives knew that the pop-up club would have been at a warehouse, so they began their search of the desolate downtown buildings. They utilized a black light to examine the outside of the buildings, desperately searching for the symbol that would show the mark that matched the ink on their victim.

Approaching one of the last buildings, Donahue sighed, exhausted.

"If this isn't it, then I'm calling it a night."

He shone the black light onto the brick building, scanning from left to right across the outside walls. Finally on the upper right side of the main entrance door, the beam of violet light illuminated a hidden symbol. It was the same symbol that was inked into the back of the victim's hand.

"Looks like we might have found our crime scene," Ellis announced, relieved the day wasn't a complete wash.

"Thank Christ."

The door was locked, but that wasn't anything a bullet couldn't fix. With a single shot, the metal buckle lock fell to the ground. The two detectives entered the abandoned building without so much as a raised eyebrow from the rest of the outside world. A stray bullet, breaking and entering—these were things that were easy to overlook in this part of town.

Despite there still being some daylight left burning in the sky, it would soon be dark. Furthermore, there were way too many nooks and crannies for surprises to be hiding in. Many of the areas in this warehouse were far out of the reach of the sunshine that filtered in through the high factory windows, some of which were broken out, others coated in years of dust and grime.

They each turned on their flashlight, instinctively holding it over their gun hand to guide their path around the building. While neither of the detectives was the jumpy type, they had both been on the force long enough to know it was better to be prepared than to walk into an unknown situation blind and unarmed.

The makeshift club was damp and musty. Evidence of the party held the night before was scattered around the large, empty warehouse floor in the forms of condom wrappers, plastic cups, and old burned-out glow sticks. The familiar scent of lubricant and candle wax still hung in the air, as well as the stale odor of spilt beer that had seeped into the concrete floor.

"Looks like one hell of a party," Donahue murmured as he kicked an empty plastic cup across the floor, sending it skittering across the concrete. In the abandoned building the noise was deafening.

The detectives examined the building from top to bottom, but, without suitable lighting, their walk-through was cursory at best. They agreed to send the crime scene techs out in the morning; hopefully they would find something they couldn't see.

Chapter Seven

Sleep did not come easily to Detective Ellis that night. As his unconscious mind roamed freely, images from the day fluttered behind his closed eyelids.

In his dream, he wandered into a dark club. It was like many others he had visited in his youth. Finding his roots, meeting new people, practicing his Dominant nature; these clubs served many purposes for him. This one appeared to be just like the rest: dimly lit, well attended, and equipped with bondage furniture and toys on the wall.

Beneath one of the spotlights in the room, he saw a mane of blonde hair weave in and out of the crowd. The golden strands echoed so many of the girls in his past, but held an ethereal quality that especially captured his attention. Something familiar yet distant stirred inside of him, a feeling only dreams could conjure from your defenses, dormant in the unconscious realm.

He followed this glowing golden beauty, pushing through the sea of club goers clad in black leather or PVC, others nude and leashed at their Top's feet. Whenever he thought he was getting close enough to place a hand on the delicate shoulder of the stranger, the crowd would shift and swallow her up, and she would advance before him, her thin frame draped in black satin, eluding him again and again.

As he followed her, she skirted the edges of the spotlight. The light was no longer capturing her golden strands or glistening off of the soft fabric of her spaghetti-strapped cocktail dress. She then exited through a door, and panic set into his chest as he lost all sight of her.

He tried to push his way through the crowd, but they resisted his forceful gestures to part them. The wall of flesh thickened around him and the air began to become hot, thick, and heavy. Then, suddenly, the club was gone and he was standing in a forest.

The entire atmosphere changed, and he was aware in the way only lucid dreaming could offer the dreamer. He still wore his basic attire of black jeans, boots, and a black tee that fit his athletic build perfectly, but his feet were now planted firmly in overgrown grass and dead leaves that had fallen from the trees above him, instead of the concrete floor of the club he had just been in.

An Indian summer's leftover humidity and the cool breeze of the new autumn made his skin stick and glisten with a thin layer of perspiration, and then chilled him in an uncontrollable shiver. The change in atmosphere made his head swim dizzily, and a feeling of familiarity grew within him. He suddenly forgot his blonde-haired beauty and wanted to wake up as the feeling grew and an unprovoked panic set in.

However, his brain would not let him leave his dream. In his unconscious realm, despite his adamancy to awaken from this dream, he moved through the forest. His feet appeared to move one step after another, without listening to his own intentions.

The crunching of the dead leaves beneath his feet signified the summer had passed, and now he could smell the scent of death from the fallen and rotten foliage littering the forest floor. The musky scent of mold and decay filled his nostrils.

Somewhere in the back of his memory, the scent of formaldehyde was triggered. Both scents were vividly real to him at the moment, and, in a strange way, the coroner's chemical now accompanied the scent of vegetation's death as a back note in the recesses of his nasal passage. His dream and reality were beginning to mix in a way that made him extremely uneasy. He wanted to wake up. He was desperate to wake up.

In the last rays of the dying sunlight, now settling beneath the horizon for the evening, he saw a twinkling of gold along the forest floor. The rays of natural light were receding, and intermittent spurts of solar rays caught everything in sight, illuminating like gold in sparks of fire, like a lightening bug signaling to its mate to come closer. Smaller, more intense twinkling came just inches from where the gold flashed, also in response to the sunlight. These were more like twinkling stars than fire, like tiny fairy lights.

The dancing of the lights captivated Ellis as he made his way closer to the source. His eyes never left the object casting the golden sparks as his feet moved over roots, snapping twigs beneath his weight. He was now mere feet away, and he stretched out his hand to move the low-hanging tree branches that separated him from the subject of his persistent interest, always just out of his reach. While nothing was pursuing him or pressing him to move on, a feeling of dread lumped in his throat. He felt as if he could no longer swallow, and his breath caught heavily in his chest. He began to pull the branches back, but before his eyes could see the object of his investigation, he awoke in his bed.

Sweat poured down his face, and his bed sheets were now soaked with the perspiration of unspoken and unbeknownst fear. He gasped a breath in through his mouth. It felt like the first one he had taken since he entered the woods in his dream realm. He panted heavily and felt his heart jackrabbit in his chest. He was having a panic attack.

He violently removed the blankets and covers from the bed and ran to the bathroom, his feet barely able to feel the cold wooden floor beneath him as his head swam. He lifted the toilet seat and vomited into the bowl as soon as he lowered himself on the tile floor.

Sweat poured down his face, fear still pressed on his chest, and he lowered his head into the porcelain to hurl again. He could have sworn he smelled the scent of rot and decay exit his nose as he purged the contents from his stomach—the smell of death.

Finally he hit the lever on the toilet, then rocked back on his feels and leaned against the wall. The cool tile bathroom floor and wall pressed against his hot and clammy skin. Finally his heartbeat was starting to settle back down in his chest, but the burn from his sudden vomiting still lit his throat on fire. It hurt to breathe, both in his throat as well as his strained lungs.

He squeezed his eyes closed and leaned his head back, mopping the back of his hand across his forehead and wiping away the sweat from his cheeks. The dreams and thoughts still lingered in his mind's eye, but were becoming distant and cloudy the longer he was awake, the way dreams lost their sharpness as the gravity of reality set in.

Chapter Eight

Ellis awoke early the next morning, just as the sun was beginning to brighten the fading night sky. He had a strong hankering for a drink, a feeling he had been battling with since his sobriety began nearly a decade ago. While he was usually able to stave off the beast and keep him at bay, he found it clutching his willpower tightly this morning, tighter than usual, and suffocating the self-control he had taught himself over the years.

His parched tongue stuck to the roof of his mouth as he rolled over in his linen-free bed. Images from the dreamscapes of the night before still ran through his mind in sporadic flashes, and not even in the order they originally occurred. Some images seemed like real memories, while others felt like past images from television shows he had once watched as a child.

The sour taste of vomit was still bitter in the back of his mouth, despite having brushed his teeth once he'd collected himself off of the bathroom floor. The strange leftover feelings of Domination and submission in one person mingled within him. Could his dreams have been about Celeste and his inklings that she was indeed a switch? But why would this bother him now? And why was there such a strong overtone of death?

Being a switch was not something society embraced. If one couldn't decide, then they wanted it all, and in order to keep a society that thrived off of instant gratification and pleasure, there had to be certain safeguards in place.

It was commonly found in many examples of the past that switches tend to be uncontrollably hedonistic in their pleasure. They wanted what they wanted, when they wanted it, and this sometimes led to unsafe and even dangerous decisions.

Ellis admitted it to himself, and only himself, that he and his blue-eyed girl shared these compulsions, but he was always in control of every situation between them. Why should such primal actions be looked down upon? Since he'd been an inexperienced young man, he couldn't remember a single bad decision or misstep he had made in the scene with a partner, yet now the topic plagued him and he couldn't get back to sleep as it nagged uncontrollably at his thoughts.

***

In a decision that was mostly made from sleep deprivation and desperation, Ellis called Donahue to meet him at the coffee shop they sometimes grabbed breakfast at. Perhaps it was a ridiculously early hour, but he needed someone to talk to, and Donahue was the only one he trusted.

Walking into the diner, the bells chimed above the door to announce his entrance. Despite being a 24/7 diner, there were only a handful of other patrons scattered around the booths and long counter in the front, where a few waitresses hovered refilling coffee cups and sliding plates in front of hungry patrons. Seeing the potential audience, Ellis began to regret picking this establishment as their meeting place.

Fifties doo-wop music escaped the speakers, and the neon colors assaulted his tired and restless eyes. Perhaps this diner wasn't the wisest choice at all.

Themed diners that catered to fantasies of women in the past had begun to pop up in the last couple of decades. This one was a retro 1950s-style diner with girls in poodle skirts and saddle shoes. However, unlike the historical clothing of the time, these girls hemmed their skirts ridiculously short, and many of them found black and white heels instead of the traditional flat saddle shoes that debuted in the era. Sex was timeless, and, despite the era, sex always sold—and these girls were selling it very, very well.

Ellis couldn't say he minded this. There was something so naturally submissive about this time in the past, and the look of the era made the Dominant inside of him hungry. But today sex wasn't the first thing on his weary mind.

However, one waitress in particular caught his attention—a cute young brunette with long hair put up into a high ponytail. Her bubblegum-pink lipstick matched her temptingly short poodle skirt. The white petticoat beneath it flared the skirt out around her small waist.

Pulling his attention from the pretty young thing, he scanned the restaurant for his partner. He wasn't surprised at all to see him already there waiting in a booth, despite the fact that Ellis had arrived five minutes early.

His nickname for Donahue of "Mr. Punctuality" fluttered through his mind once again as he took a seat opposite him at the table. His partner already had a cup of coffee in front of him, and who knew if it was his first. The staff here was quick to refill, and, just as this thought occurred, the waitress had already sauntered over and was flipping his coffee mug upright onto the saucer and filling it brim-high.

He looked up to see it was the young waitress whom he'd made eyes with earlier at the door. As she stood closer now, he could fully appreciate the white polo she wore, unbuttoned halfway to expose her cleavage. Yet even more tempting was the fact that she wore a pink and white polka-dotted scarf tied delicately around her neck. His eyes stayed transfixed as she finished the task of pouring his coffee, and apparently she had said something he'd completely missed, as Donahue answered for him.

"No, thanks, just coffee for now."

Even though it was Donahue who spoke, she let her eyes linger for an extra moment on the detective, which he fully appreciated. She then turned with the flash of a pearly white smile for the men and left their table.

Ellis wasn't sure if it was because they were becoming regulars, or because she was working extra hard this morning for tips, but he certainly enjoyed the attention. The sad fact was many of these waitresses were part of the tertiary tier, and not only did they work hard for tips, they also worked hard for new partners.

"Not much sleep last night?" Donahue asked as his partner took a long sip of his black coffee.

"Is it that obvious?" Ellis asked, rubbing the heel of his palm against his temple.

Donahue shrugged and followed it with a sip from his own coffee, which appeared to be heavy on the cream this morning. "Not sure if it's obvious, or if I'm just a good detective." He grinned as he settled the mug back into its corresponding saucer.

Ellis offered a small amused curl of his lips in return, but the joke fell flat on him. Images from the night before still flooded his mind. Most were blurred around the edges, but some, the ones that disturbed him the most, were still sharp as day. The image that stuck most with him was the moment he was about to pull back the tree branches and discover what the source of his fear finally was. Even now it made his heart catch in his throat.

"What's on your mind, Wes?"

Donahue only used his first name when it was serious. The sound of it pulled the distracted detective from his thoughts and back to the present.

"What made you wake me up on my day off and get me out of bed at six a.m. for a shitty cup of coffee?"

Ellis glanced around the diner, gesturing to the establishment in a nonchalant twirl of his hand. "What's the matter, Donahue? Don't like the décor?"

From the corner of his eye, he saw a particularly young and attractive young waitress catch his gesture, mistaking it for him appreciating her, and offer Ellis a smile that would harden any man's cock. If it was any other time, he would probably have taken her up on it. He begrudgingly removed his gaze and focused back on the conversation at hand.

His partner was stoic and silent. He was not amused.

With an internal sigh of defeat, the grey-haired detective finally let out what had been on his mind.

"Do you ever wonder why we put away switches?" He immediately braced himself for the response he knew was coming, and he was right to.

"Christ, Wes, is this what we're here to talk about? Switches?"

In his peripheral, he could sense some patrons turn their attention to their table at the mere word. The thought crossed Ellis's mind again that this wasn't the best place to talk about the topic at hand, but it was too late now.

His silence was all Donahue needed to confirm his question; this was indeed the reason he had dragged him out of bed on his day off— his day off that was supposed to be dedicated to his wife and kids. His pregnant wife who was so close to delivering his third child any time now. He sighed again.

"What is there to talk about? They're nut jobs. Wackos."

"But what if they're not?" Ellis quickly countered, and instantly he put it together in his mind that he was indeed talking about Celeste. He wanted to justify his attraction to her, especially if he discovered without a doubt that she was a switch.

"What are you talking about?"

"We have put away just as many Dominants and submissives who have committed heinous acts as we have those who claim to play on both sides of the slash. Just hear me out—"

"No!" His partner unexpectedly cut him off firmly as he brought a closed fist down on the table between them. Both of their coffee cups clattered in the glass saucers they rested in.

Once again Ellis felt eyes make their way over to their table, and the room seemed to hush for one long, brief moment. His partner seemed to make this observation as well, and let a moment pass to catch his temper. He met the eyes of some of the patrons whose attention had been briefly pulled toward their booth, and as his eyes found theirs, they returned to their own affairs, one by one.

This was not the morning Ellis had expected, and this certainly wasn't the scene he had planned to make.

His partner lowered his closed fist and then lowered his voice, but the intensity in his voice remained. "No, I will not hear you out, and do you know why? Because this conversation is ridiculous! You can't argue with years of psychological research, recidivism rates, and concrete cases that you yourself have witnessed that support the fact that those who can't choose between Topping and bottoming are more likely to be unstable than your average Dom or sub. They're risk takers, and, most of the time, those risks only cater to their own selfish satisfaction—and they don't pay off."

Ellis was silent as he knew his partner had more to say, but what came next stunned him.

"My sister was killed by a guy who claimed to be submissive to her, just her. He stated he lived for her, loved her, but in the heat of the moment he turned on her. He wanted to know what it felt like to be on Top for once. He got too rough, and hit her head on the edge of a nightstand. She bled out before the ambulance could even arrive."

Ellis was silent. He wanted to apologize, to take back everything he had said to spare his partner having to relive this memory, but he couldn't help but think this could have been attributed to so many other variables: a freak accident, a miscommunication in events, a mistake on her part. However, these were not the things his partner wanted to hear. He could tell from the tone in his voice and the look in his eye, one which he had never seen before, that he had made up his mind about what had happened, and nothing would sway him otherwise.

"So, no, Wes, I will not listen to you," Donahue concluded as he got to his feet, tossing enough cash on the table to cover both of their coffees and tip before making his departure. "Not about this."

Chapter Nine

Nearly a week had passed since the two detectives had searched the impromptu club, and not a single lead had surfaced. Well, Ellis technically couldn't say that. Once they'd put Yvonne's picture out on the news, the department had received an onslaught of calls, and while each one was followed up on, none of them panned out to be of any use.

He had worked with his partner since their heated debate at the diner, and their working relationship, as well as their friendship, hadn't seemed to take a hit. If it had, Donahue was a very good liar and hadn't revealed any of it. However, that is how men were. They fought; they moved on.

With the days being filled with one dead end lead after another, Ellis wished he could say his time away from the job was anything but boring. However, it wasn't. He hadn't heard from his blue-eyed girl in over a week now, and his hunger for her began to grow with each day.

While he could go out to any club or party and return to his apartment with a girl, or even two, for a play session or a good fuck, that could only offer so much, especially as he was getting older.

With each grey hair that newly sprouted, he felt as if the meaningless sex he'd had in the days of his past, and the girls he had made scream beneath his skilled hands, were less and less fulfilling. They would spread their legs or take their pain from anyone who would show an interest. What he really wanted, yet he didn't want to admit it to himself, was the dedication and the servitude of someone who saw him, and only him, as their world.

He knew Celeste could never be this for him, but she was the closest he had tasted in years to this kind of dedication, and this made him wonder if his yearning to see her was something more than just the hedonism they shared for each other.

These thoughts intermingled with the intense and unrelenting dreams he had been having. Never in the dreamscapes that had passed with each night had the identity of his golden-haired beauty been revealed to him, but it always left him with a feeling of dread and intrigue, and a hungry passion that made his cock hard. Each day when he awoke in the early hours of the morning, many times before the sun itself would even rise, his cock was pulsating with a life of its own.

Much to his surprise, one morning he noticed he had ejaculated in his sleep. His stomach and sheets around him were sticky and wet with fresh cum. He hadn't had a wet dream since adolescence, and if he hadn't been alone, he'd have felt ashamed of his cock's betrayal. Yet all he felt in the quiet still of the morning was a murky sense of pleasure and bewilderment.

There was something about these dreams that had a firm hold on him, somewhere between the lines of terror and pleasure, enough so that his cock discharged a healthy amount of cum without a single stroke from his hand.

Despite how many times he dreamt of this subject matter, he never understood what exactly he was dreaming of that made him feel this way. Or who. It always felt somewhere between the world of fantasy and reality.

Of course he had his suspicions, but even his blue-eyed girl didn't spark this mixture of feelings inside of him. He never feared her. He never felt as if he wasn't in control of their romps and scenes. However, the lack of control he felt in this dream realm was unnerving, and as a man who was always calm, cool, and collected, he was beginning to feel the first slip of his grip on reality, and he did not like it. Not one bit.

Chapter Ten

It was a week later when a call went out to the two men that another body had been found inside an apartment. Apparently the neighbor had seen the door open, and entered to check on the occupant and made the gruesome discovery.

To his shock, he arrived at the crime scene before Donahue. What were the chances of that? The location of the homicide was an old factory that had been newly renovated into lofts. It was in the secondary sector, and apparently a well-off section of it that teetered the primary line. However, there was no doorman here, and the video camera at the entrance was not working.

Typical. When you were a detective, it usually felt like the powers that be commonly worked against you to make your life that much more difficult in effectively performing your job.

Before he stepped over the threshold, Ellis examined the door that led into the apartment. There were no obvious signs of a break-in. The door frame remained unbroken and intact, the doorknob wasn't bashed in, nor had the lock been tampered with. There wasn't even the scuff of a boot mark on the face of the door itself to indicate a forced entry. It was apparent the vic knew their assailant, or the perpetrator had been very persuasive in manipulating themselves into the apartment.

One of the boys in blue lifted the crime scene tape for Ellis. The detective always found it interesting how a single piece of yellow tape could effectively close off the scene from the outside world, and in this case the apartment from the hallway.

He offered the detective a respectful nod, and Ellis returned the gesture before ducking under the tape.

The red and blue lights from the police cars outside streamed in through the large renovated factory windows. Their glaring glow illuminated the loft in the two harsh primary colors which bounced and glared off of the framed art hanging around the expansive room, which apparently served as both a bedroom and the main living quarters. To his left, still cloaked in darkness and just out of reach of the police lights, was probably the kitchen and bathroom.

He had heard some of the cops talking outside over cigarettes and coffee. They were supposed to be making sure no one except law enforcement entered the building. Ellis rolled his eyes at their ineffectiveness.

Upon his arrival, he'd heard them mutter something about the vic being a big deal. Looking around at the art on the walls, he wondered if this is what they meant. Without the lights on, he couldn't tell if she was the model or the photographer, but he could make out the silhouette of a slenderly built, mostly naked female subject in various positions in all of the frames.

The loft was clean and free of a struggle. The couch pillows, the magazines on the coffee table, and even the glass of wine resting on the nightstand next to the bed were all undisturbed. This led him to believe it was a play session gone wrong, or rough sex gone bad. Perhaps even drugs had been involved to sedate the victim. In their world, drugs to relax the body during a play scene weren't uncommon, particularly if the Top was into medical fetish, or even the taboo interest of necrophilia. *Doc Jensen will love this case,* Ellis thought darkly.

The detective made a mental note to check the bathroom for a bathtub filled with ice water. This was a common technique used to lower the body temperature so the bottom felt cold to the Top's touch. This would help the Top become aroused if their kink was indeed intertwined with deceased bodies.

The detective's eyes were slowly adjusting to the lack of light, but he still stepped carefully and watched where each of his foot falls landed on the hardwood floor. He wore disposable cloth footies as he padded softly along the floor. They covered his dress shoes. They were meant to capture any evidence that may have been on the ground, as well as prevent him from cross-contaminating the scene from his own shoe prints or any particles that may have been embedded in the treads.

However, as he lightly stepped around the room, he still wanted to be as careful as possible to preserve any of the evidence that may have been left, which, to his dismay, appeared to be very little. Hopefully the crime scene investigators would be able to work their magic and find some fingerprints, or hair and fiber evidence.

It was hard to process a crime scene in these dimly lit conditions. The shadows cast on the walls from the police car lights were playing tricks on his eyes, not to mention being extremely distracting.

"Where's the damned lights?" he barked over to the cop at the door.

"The company is trying to get them back on now, sir."

"Christ," he muttered to himself as he inched closer to the bed.

The lights on top of the cop cars cast an eerie glow on the bed, where the body lay dormant and lifeless. She was tied spread-eagled on the bed, each of her limbs connected to one of the four bedposts with rope. He could see the rope was most likely jute, a coarse, fibrous material that bit into the skin and left rope burn much more easily than the softer nylon rope.

The flashing red and blue lights reflected on the blood that had pooled on the ground, indicating that at least one cut had severed an artery, as well as the thick coat that had long begun to coagulate and form a shiny, sticky layer on the left side of the victim's face. Blood also gathered at various other areas of her body, where injuries had broken the skin and released blood which now appeared black in the absence of any adequate lighting.

Slowly approaching the bedside, careful not to step in any of the blood or castoff spray, Ellis pulled on a pair of latex medical gloves. He visually examined the woman. She wore a man's shirt, unbuttoned and revealing a blood-smeared torso. It was hard to tell if the source of blood was from one cut or many. Maybe it was just overflow from another wound; there was really no way to tell at this time. In fact, there was no way to tell most of the details right now. He'd faced a lot of challenging crime scenes before, but detecting in the dark? *Give me a fucking break*, he thought.

The fact that she was wearing a man's shirt led him to believe she'd been dressed post mortem. The shirt was not clean by any means, but the only blood staining it came from contact the material had made with her already beaten and bloodied body, seemingly after her injuries had been inflicted.

She must have been killed on the bed, in the nude, and then dressed by the assailant. But for what reason? He had seen bodies covered in bedsheets or blankets, or even just the head covered in a t-shirt as an act of remorse on the perpetrator's part, but to be dressed in an oversize man's button-down shirt, post mortem, was something new to him. There was something artificial about it. It was almost theatrical.

Yet somewhere in the back of his brain, it was familiar. Perhaps he had seen it in another case before. In twenty years, he had seen a lot of things, and he would have to pore back over his past cases to try and find a connection.

The restraints binding her wrists and ankles to the bedposts all appeared to have been cut from the same length of rope. From the foot of the bed, he observed her head resting on the white cotton pillow which was now stained with blood.

As he approached closely, he noticed it was also littered with pieces of something. Watching his steps, he moved even closer until with his gloved fingers he could pick up a piece from the soft cotton linen. Holding it close to his eyes, he could now see what it was—hair. He placed it back on the pillow. Whoever killed her had also cut off her hair.

With his eyes continuing to adjust to the dimly lit loft, he was beginning to pick up on some of the smaller details. Ellis could now see that some of the locks of hair were clotted with blood as they lay strewn about the top half of the bed. Other pieces were untouched by the blood, still soft and smooth to the touch.

In the red and blue strobe of the lights, her closed eyelids appeared to offer a small glitter. He leaned closer, hoping this wasn't what it appeared to be.

Suddenly the overhead lights came on, momentarily shooting a glaring pain into his eyes and throughout his head. With a groan, he tightly closed his them against the bright fluorescents.

"Lights are on," the cop matter-of-factly informed him from the doorway.

"Thanks," Ellis muttered through clenched teeth.

His irritation and annoyance quickly dissolved once he opened his eyes. He let the spots fade from his vision, and, when he was able to focus, he could see with sharp clarity the gruesome crime scene on the bed, and who was lying there.

The victim he had been sharing the room with for the past fifteen minutes, the woman whom he had nearly been eye-to-eye with just moments ago, was someone he knew. This was a redhead from his past, and was indeed someone he was very well acquainted with.

It was his first serious partner in the scene. Someone he had played with when they were just stupid kids right out of school, before he had entered the police academy.

Forgetting it was a crime scene, he blindly backed up against the floor-to-ceiling windows behind him. When he couldn't retreat from the bed any further, he slid down to the floor, eyes fixated on the body splayed out on the bed. No, not just a body, not just a victim, not anymore. Now that the lights were on, she now had an identity. She had a name—Tina.

A cold sweat immediately broke out along his forehead and he rocked his head backwards, hitting the window behind him with a solid thud. The collision mixed with the shock made a deafening ringing in his ears, and he felt like he was going to vomit from the sheer volume of it inside his head.

He frantically grabbed at his tie, his fingers working blindly at the knot. They clumsily loosened the fabric noose from around his neck. He couldn't work fast enough to get air into his lungs, which were now constricting tightly with fear and horror.

He ripped off his suit jacket as well, tossing it to the floor. He felt the cold air from outside the glass pane against the heat radiating from his head, and now along his back, right through his button-down shirt. Without thinking, he ran his gloved hands through his hair; beads of perspiration were already collecting along his hairline and his face. In a matter of seconds, he had tainted the crime scene worse than a rookie cop, but his brain was not functioning as a detective at the moment— it was functioning as a man who had discovered his friend had been violently killed and was just two inches in front of him.

"You ok, Detective?" the cop from the doorway called. Seeing the seasoned detective had crumbled to the ground, the cop had lifted the crime scene tape and was about to enter the apartment.

"Yeah, fine," he gasped, trying to get a handle on himself. Seeing the cop was about to come to his aid, he held up his gloved hand, now streaked in sweat, to stop him.

"Don't! Stay there!" he barked. "I'm fine." He breathed deeply. "Just keep the press out." He tried to regain some semblance of composure.

He painfully realized that, if the cop hadn't broken through his thought process, he would have been falling headlong into a panic attack spiral.

The young officer just nodded and stepped back to maintain his post, but as fate would have it, Donahue rounded the corner just then. His eyes widened, initially at the sight on the bed that Ellis hadn't even had time to fully take in once the lights had gone on. His eyes then practically exploded out of his head when he saw his partner on the ground, pushed up against the windows.

"Christ, Wes!" he exclaimed from the door and ducked under the tape to run to his side. "Are you ok?"

"Yeah," he muttered reluctantly. He just wanted a moment to himself, but he wasn't going to get that. He had to gather his composure quickly and sort through these feelings later.

Donahue crouched down to his partner's level and evaluated his face, not with the scrutiny of a detective, but with the concern of a friend.

"What happened?"

Whatever rivalry the two men had debated about weeks earlier in the coffee shop had certainly slipped away. The only thing in his partner's eyes, besides concern, was a glimmer of fright, as he had never seen Wes in such a state of disarray before.

"I know her," he said, motioning with a nod to the bed, but his eyes remained on the floor. "The vic, I know her." His voice was soft as he waited for the ringing in his ears to subside. The urge to hurl was still there, but was slowly dissipating as his breathing began to regulate back to normal.

Donahue looked up at the bloody mess covering the large bed. "Oh shit, man, I'm sorry." He helped his partner get back to his feet. "Are you ok? Do you want me to work this one alone?"

"No, no," he quickly replied. "I—I just didn't expect it to be someone I know. Knew."

"I'm sure you didn't. Who would?" He looked over his partner, who was now facing the windows, away from the bed. "And in that condition … Fuck, I'm sorry man." Donahue repeated himself; he obviously didn't know where to go past an apology.

Ellis was about to turn back to the scene, but Donahue steadied him with his hands to look in his partner's face. "Are you *sure* you want to do this?"

Ellis nodded slowly. "Yeah."

Traditionally, in the old days anyhow, a detective would be pulled off the case if they knew the victim, especially if they were related to them. However, these days it was so frequent to be acquainted with someone in the world where casual play and one night stands were commonplace. It was also hard to find a good detective to do the job, so that rule had long been lifted.

While Ellis had known a vic or two through being an acquaintance, he had never known a victim as intimately as he had Tina. While this didn't make him not want to work the case, it didn't make him giddy to do so either.

The least he could do was catch the son of a bitch who'd done this to her. He readied himself to take in the scene, now that the overhead lights were working. Breathing deeply, he turned back to face her, and he was able to see exactly what had been done to the redhead.

Chapter Eleven

As Ellis had deducted, her once long and lustrous red locks were now cut and scattered about the linen and pillows. The same hair he had pulled as he rode her ass, and then caressed gently and ran his fingers through delicately after fucking her.

Her eyes were closed, and the way the blood on her face had rolled along the curves of her cheeks made it look as if she was crying tears of blood. They had cascaded down her milky, pale face and frozen there permanently as they coagulated and stained her skin. Her beautiful, youthful face was now forever frozen in a state of sadness, and she would always be weeping those crimson tears.

A garrote was tied around her neck. It appeared to have been made out of fishing wire and a short cane, known in their world as an evil stick. It was hard to tell if asphyxiation was the cause of death, as her body was battered and broken with injuries in so many areas. The garrote could have just been torture leading up to a different means of death. The amount of blood at the scene suggested blood loss as the cause of her demise, but it was impossible tell from which wound.

Despite the obvious, there was something wrong about seeing Tina lying here like this, beaten and bloodied. It seemed almost like a personal attack, not against her body, rather against who she was as a person.

The cutting of her hair had dismantled her beauty, and that was obvious to any detective. However, knowing her personally, Ellis remembered that she could take a beating and not bat an eyelash. She was the first true pain slut he had ever met.

Tina was the one who'd not only opened him up to knowing what he wanted from the scene, but had also helped him feel at ease with it. She'd taught him to embrace his sadism and not let it make him feel like a monster. As a young man, this had been a constant battle in his head for many reasons, and she had helped quiet those demons enough to deal with them. Temporarily, at least.

He was a sadist at heart, and she a masochist. Her cravings for pain had made him her perfect fit. She'd given him an outlet for his form of Dominant play, and, because of his style, he'd been the only one at the time who could fulfill her requests and masochistic nature.

To have been tortured like this at the hands of someone who knew her limits and had slowly pushed her past them, one by one—it made his stomach turn. It was degrading. She had deserved better than this. She had deserved to die with dignity. Instead, she had been tortured to death, literally.

The marks from the wire cut deeply into her throat, and some were even encrusted with dried blood along the thin lines the implement had made. If this was indeed the main cause of death, the perpetrator had not let her slip away upon the first tightening of the device. It was clear he had repeatedly choked her, again and again.

Seeing the wire cut through her skin was agonizing for Ellis. This method didn't even register on his chart as an asphyxiation aficionado. He preferred using his hands because it was precise and personal. This, on the other hand, was cold and detached from any sort of passion. It was grotesque and cruel.

The coroner would be able to tell him how deep the wire had cut, but on a personal level he did not want to know, because he knew Tina would have felt every second of it.

Below her neck, he could now see the source of the blood that had pooled along her torso. It came from three long gashes along her abdomen. With all of the blood, it was hard to see where they began and ended, as well as how many wounds there were in total. There could have easily been more than three, but that was what he could see at the moment.

Knowing how much blood a person could lose before bleeding out, none of them appeared life threatening, but the doc would know for sure. And while it appeared she had lost an awful lot of blood, part of that was the illusion, since everything had been white and was now stained red.

It looked like a slaughterhouse. However, blood easily spread and soaked into fabrics, crawling across the material and seeping into the thirsty pores like fresh winter snow. A single drop of blood could have spread out to cover the area of a quarter.

The detective studied Tina's body. Bruises discolored her pure white skin in various shades of pinks and purples. The perp's M.O. appeared to be to torture the girl rather than bring about a quick death. It was as if he wanted to see how much pain she could really take before he finally let her retreat into the sweet escape of death. This was a true monster.

"What was her name?" Donahue asked, pulling Ellis unwillingly from his thoughts.

"What?" he asked, as his memories and deductions of the crime scene faded and the present moment of the room came rushing back in.

"Her name. What was it?"

"Tina, Tina Nolan." Her collar bearing an initial was nowhere to be seen. It wasn't on her delicate and now mutilated neck, or on her pillow or bed stand beside her. Giving the floor a quick cursory glance, he didn't see it there, either. The crime scene investigators would find it if it was in the apartment, but something told Ellis it was gone, just like Yvonne's.

Now, as he looked around the room, he was able to see it was indeed Tina in all of the pictures framed and proudly displayed around the loft. She had become a famous model since the days he knew her. In all of her pictures, she wore her gold chain accompanied by her lower-case initial "t." Ellis motioned for Donahue to follow his eyes to the photographs.

"Let's find out who else was in her life. Ask the neighbors what they know. A lot of the time, models wear their submissive collars even after being owned. It helps them portray the image of being available."

"You got it." He gently clapped a hand on his partner's shoulder in a last ditch effort of comfort, then left the room quietly. Ellis was glad he had taken the cue that he needed to be alone to finish processing the crime scene.

Ellis walked the parameter of the large living area, examining each picture carefully. It was hard to tell if she still practiced and played regularly in the scene, or what form her kinks may have taken since their dynamic ended decades ago. To Ellis now, it seemed like a lifetime ago.

With the advances in post-production photography, makeup, and surgeries, her body looked as smooth and virginal as it did before he ever placed his first marks upon it all of those years ago.

Running his eyes back over her nude body, he now saw in the artificial light that her ankles and wrists were red and rubbed raw. It was from where she had pulled and tugged against the ropes that had confined her movements. Tina was a fighter, and he knew she would have struggled against these ropes until they broke, or broke her. In fact, the rope, which was once a pure white nylon, was now coated with her blood. It had long dried and had turned dark red and brown, but each place where she had been bound held these blood stains. She had put up a good fight.

Leaning in closely to see the knots used to bind her wrists, Ellis discovered a hair trapped beneath a fingernail on her left hand.

"Did you get a piece of him?" he asked as he removed a tube to collect the specimen. With tweezers he carefully picked up the single hair, root intact, and placed it into the tube where he sealed it closed to keep it from being contaminated by the outside elements. "Good girl," he whispered.

This simple two-worded phrase was something he had said to her so many times before in the past—times when she had pleased him, as well as times when he'd shown genuine affection—a past that seemed so long ago, and only felt distantly familiar. He thought to himself, sadly, this would be the last time he would ever get to say these words to her.

Chapter Twelve

Tina's Story

Tina was a fiery redhead of only eighteen when Ellis had met her, and he was just two years her senior. It was the summer between high school and college, and life was so full of possibilities and opportunities for them, especially Tina.

Tina was an aspiring model. Well, "aspiring" wasn't really the right word when you had been gracing websites and then later adult advertisements since your young teenage years. She was born with the uncanny ability to never reveal her true age, as if she had sprung from the fountain of youth itself.

No matter how she wore her hair and clothes, she appealed to every tier of their society. Her beauty was limitless, and her personality elegant and refined. All of this is probably why she never struggled finding work. However, despite her obviously growing success and potential, she never let it go to her head.

On the other hand, the life that Ellis was leading at the time was very different. Despite being in the secondary tier where life was comfortable, with many doors opened to advancement, he knew his own path was predestined. Since he was a young boy, he knew he would follow in the footsteps of his father and go into law enforcement.

Tina, on the other hand, had a natural gift of beauty and grace, and she was pure magic in front of a camera. Whether it was for photograph, film, or stage, she was always the person everyone's eyes went to. For having such a gift, she never flaunted her looks, and she never let it cause her to act superior to anyone. This was one of the things Ellis liked most about her.

She also had a passion for life like no one he had ever met before, and her green eyes lit up with an enthusiasm and spirit that was unparalleled to most he would meet in the future. This look in her eye begged for him to tame her, beneath him as a submissive, and the desire he felt to do so was relentless. Once he saw her, he knew he had to have her.

Unlike many of the women, and especially men, who admired the young redhead, her beauty didn't make her a prize to him. He was raised to believe beauty was secondary to being a willing submissive. However, bringing out her submission and molding it beneath him certainly was a worthy prize for the young man who'd only had limited experience with long-term submissives up until this point.

She would prove to be his first successful submissive that was a match to his own style and needs as a Top. It wasn't until her that he felt his inner sadist could be satisfied and mostly unrestricted.

They frequented dungeons, clubs, and parties, and it was neither secret nor surprise that when they played all eyes went to them. While Ellis let it go to his head more than Tina, he still kept himself calm and collected and didn't let it interfere with his style, nor did he let it take his attention from her mid-scene. His bottom's safety was always his primary concern, and if their interactions drew a crowd, then so be it—they could watch.

No matter what they did—impact play, rope work, protocol—all of it was magical between them. They had an unspoken connection that displayed what Tops and bottoms wanted in their own dynamics. The way they interacted with another and moved in tune to each other's actions, outsiders would think the two were in love. Yet that wasn't it. Not in the slightest.

Despite how much he felt Tina was his equal as well as his match in so many ways, love was never a factor in it. He had loved only once before her, and none since then. Later in life, he considered himself incapable of it, but not until his later years did that begin to bother him.

The time they shared together was some of the most important growth Ellis had experienced as a Dominant. She fully submitted to him in their physical scenes of sadism and masochism. He learned how to fully embrace a bottom's needs, physical or mental, firsthand.

As a Top, he learned how to read body language and cues from his bottom, and just as importantly the aftercare one needs in the scene. This is also where he learned that he himself as a Dominant needed aftercare. The things he did to her were so intense that he needed her reassurance that he was not a monster, and that she saw him for the person he was, the complete person, both inside their scenes and out. He needed to know she trusted him, and she did.

While the relationship came to an end naturally and Tina quickly found another Top to explore with, Ellis had stayed unattached for a while. It was hard for him to find someone who complimented him so completely, and until Celeste he never had again.

Chapter Thirteen

Just as he placed Celeste's note amongst his collection of the others in his nightstand drawer, his phone rang. Glancing at the caller ID, he sighed. Ellis rubbed the heel of his hand wearily against his forehead to try and dull the headache that felt as if it was going to split his skull in half. Hangover or not, it was time for him to get back to the real world.

"Ellis," he answered, sleep still heavy in his voice. He listened to the caller and occasionally peppered in a few one-word responses, but mostly just listened. Finally he ended the phone call with "I'll be there in an hour."

The memories of yesterday flooded back into his brain. The latest victim, Tina, was the reason he'd gone to the bar last night in the first place and was nursing this hangover this morning.

He didn't know if he had the strength to go to the coroner's office today. He had been haunted by his nightmares the night before about the same blonde-haired woman and the aimless wandering through the forest. He hadn't got any closer to identifying her, but the dream had revealed something new. This time he had reached into his pocket and found a gold chain with the letter "c" on it.

This had led him to believe that these images were indeed connected to his blue-eyed girl, but what did they mean? He didn't have time to analyze them this morning for any longer than it took him to get dressed and drive downtown, but somewhere in the back of his mind they stayed with him, waiting to be revisited.

***

Ellis never enjoyed going to the coroner's office, but this was a trip down to the basement that he was especially dreading. The only noise this morning came from his footsteps echoing back to him as he approached the third door on the right. In the distance, he could also detect the buzz of the fluorescent lights above his head, but they seemed further away than usual as his own feelings of panic, dread, and sorrow caught in his throat. Not even the scent of the dead could penetrate his somber demeanor this morning.

Entering Jensen's office, Ellis felt the bile and black coffee he had spiked with whisky just an hour ago to keep his hangover at bay start to rise in his throat. The scent that he despised so much mixed with the nausea from his hangover. The combination was just enough to nearly push him over the edge this morning. He had to swallow hard to keep it all down.

However, what instantly sobered him was the surprise he found as his eyes met Doc Jensen's. There were no two ways about it, the M.E. was visibly and exceptionally shaken. There were no perverted quips that lingered behind his lips today, nor were there any digs or jabs to verbally bust Ellis's balls. The expression on the old man's face was purely and completely vacant. He was a broken man.

"Ellis," he greeted dryly. His face had taken a sickly white complexion.

Ellis nodded just once. His eyes then went to their usual destination, the long metal table to his right across the room.

There was no bounce in the medical examiner's step this morning. In fact, he didn't even lead Ellis over there; the Detective had to walk over by himself and wait for the old man to follow. He faced him as he stood opposite across the table, waiting for his explanation that usually came so colorfully vivid and excessively detailed. Yet not this morning.

"In all my years…" he began, but he just couldn't find the words. He removed his glasses from his face and with shaky fingers cleaned them on the bottom of his white lab coat. He put them back on and pushed them up on the bridge of his nose with a slightly trembling finger.

"Doc?"

The old man looked up, startled at the sound of Ellis's voice. "Yes, well then … I'm sure you want to know what happened."

He lingered over the examination table, and for once he appeared not to be looking forward to pulling back this particular sheet—this sheet, which looked no different than any others from the outside, but held something much darker beneath.

With those same old man hands that he couldn't keep still, he revealed the body beneath the cloth. A young woman, older than their first set of victims, but certainly no older than thirty, occupied the table.

Red hair cascaded down from the crown of her head where it was parted in the middle. The length was jagged and uneven, harshly cut at different lengths and angles by hasty blades without rhyme or reason. Some pieces were cut inches from her scalp while other pieces had been left long and intact. The once beautiful head full of autumn fire had been butchered in a blind rage.

"I'll … I'll have to do something with her hair for the funeral," the doctor muttered, "and the face..."

He fumbled with his glasses again.

"That's if the family even wants an open casket."

"I don't know how they could," Ellis said under his breath as he examined the woman's appearance.

For once, the scent of the room fell away, and he was just one-on-one with this poor soul. The doc stitched up the long blade marks along her right cheek. At the crime scene, Ellis couldn't even tell how many slashes there were from the amount of blood covering her face, but now it was obvious.

Deep gashes were carved along her cleavage and breasts. They crisscrossed already-healed-over scars from prior play that were barely visible anymore, but Ellis could see them as clear as day. He would—after all, he was the one who had put them there.

He assumed the new wounds continued the entire way down, but he couldn't bring himself to lift the sheet past her navel. It would be easier to read about them in the coroner's report, rather than expose them for himself to see here and now. Both men were barely hanging on, and to reveal the entirety of Tina's wounds and suffering would have been unnecessary.

"Where to begin?" the old man said, to himself more than to Ellis. He coughed to clear his throat. "The young lady was asphyxiated, like the other victim. The crudely fashioned garrote is what cut off the oxygen to her brain, but it did more than that."

The detective's eyes traveled to Tina's neck. Now that the blood was cleaned away from her skin, he could see the multiple lines and cuts from the wire where the repeated attempts of strangulation had occurred.

He gently opened her eyes, and, to his surprise, saw that one of her eyes had been removed entirely from the socket. Before the M.E. could warn him of this, it was too late, and Ellis spun on his feet and heaved.

The sight of the missing eye was enough to finally tip him over the edge. He didn't even have time to find the nearest sink or waste basket; the floor would have to do as he hurled his morning's liquid breakfast onto the floor.

"Yeah... I meant to warn you about that," Jensen responded as he hastily grabbed a clean towel for the detective and handed it to him quietly. There was not a single word of the verbal reaming Ellis expected from the old man for puking all over his floor. Surely this was a day the doctor had been waiting for since day one, when he realized the sight and smell of the dead did not combine with Ellis's strong will or weak stomach, but the old man remained silent.

After taking the towel and composing himself, Ellis slowly leaned up. His eyes stayed adverted from the victim on the table. He tried to concentrate on a clean area of the floor and attempted to breathe evenly. He mopped at the sweat that had broken out along his face with the sleeve of his suit jacket, and attempted to regain his composure. If he wasn't busying himself with these things, he would have seen the doc's eyes were also everywhere but on the victim in front of him.

"You said on the phone you think this is the third," Ellis finally said.

"Yeah, our perp left his calling card."

"Blue Morpho dust?"

The M.E. nodded. "This time it wasn't just on her eyelids, but around her cleavage as well, around the scars on her breasts that are probably at least a decade old. Being so expensive, I wonder what made that area so special."

Ellis knew.

The doctor released a pained sigh. "It looks like we have the potential of a serial killer, Detective."

Ellis managed a nod. "With the Blue Morpho and the removal of their collars, I'd say you're right."

Christ, how was he going to explain this to his boss? It had been years since anyone had worked a serial killer case in their department. If that was indeed what this was, he knew they would need outside help, and no one in a precinct had ever welcomed the idea of having newcomers on their territory.

A long silence passed between the two men as Ellis finally allowed himself to look at Tina again. Fortunately, her eyelids had fallen back closed. She was merely a shell of the woman he remembered from so long ago.

"Detective, there's one more thing I need to tell you. I wasn't completely honest with where I found the Blue Morpho."

"It wasn't on those locations?"

"No, not it was ... but ..." he stammered. "Upon examination, I also found a whole, intact and untouched Blue Morpho butterfly in a glass vial—in the victim's vagina."

"Was she raped?"

"No, it was just placed there post mortem. Carefully. Almost like a calling card."

Ellis just nodded, running a hand through his hair that had probably turned three shades greyer between him finding the first body and this one. "Thanks for all your help, Doc," he said dryly yet sincerely before leaving the room.

Chapter Fourteen

He didn't know why, but that night he found himself at the 1950s diner he had met Donahue at earlier that week. He had wandered over to the same booth they sat at and slumped into the fake leather bench heavily, the weight of the day's events pressing heavily on him.

In a million years, he would never have suspected Tina would be a murder victim. It's the people you know who keep you from sinking too far into the black hole of this job, and when they became your job, you have nothing left. He almost felt like Tina was a casualty *because* she knew him. It was a silly thought, but one that nagged at him relentlessly.

Their parting of ways had been mutual as well as more than amicable. They had just outgrown each other, and their lives had taken them in different directions. While they'd occasionally scheduled a weekend dinner during their first year apart, it had tapered off to the occasional crossing of paths at events, and soon thereafter even less than that. While there was no ill will, Ellis would be lying to himself if he said he had thought about her at all in the last couple of years.

However, despite his lack of keeping in touch with his fiery red-haired sprite, he never wished her any animosity. In fact, when he saw her on advertisements after their breakup, he felt proud to have had such an amazing connection with her, and wished her success in all of her endeavors. It appeared her journey had taken a more private route these past couple of years, as her picture hadn't graced as many websites or businesses as it used to, but judging from her home, she was certainly still well off.

As these thoughts spiraled through his head, his coffee mug was flipped and the cup was filled. His eyes didn't notice the hand settling his cup into the saucer in front of him were accented with bubblegum-pink nails, so when he looked up to respond to the routine question of "What will it be?" he was taken aback when he saw it was the young waitress from the other day, with the polka dot scarf around her neck.

His eyes were still transfixed on her neck when she repeated her question.

"Oh, um…" He flipped aimlessly through the glossy pages of the menu, examining it like it was written in hieroglyphics. He had seen it a dozen times, but his thoughts were so scattered he looked as if it was his first.

"Just coffee?" She grinned.

He actually felt himself blush as he put the booklet of words and images down and met her gaze. "Yeah."

Her smile was warm and sincere. "I'll be around if you need a refill. Just call my name." She pointed to the embroidered "H" on the top left of her polo. "Holly." Then with a twirl of her poodle skirt, a flash of innocent white lace-trimmed panties covering an absolutely perfect ass flashed in front of his eyes before she was off to serve another table. *Was that intentional?*

Sitting in the diner, Ellis went over each of the cases again and again in his mind, desperately trying to find a connection between the girls. There had to be something he was missing that would help link him to the killer. He was too exhausted for this, and his mind wandered fruitlessly as it tried to process the information.

In mid-thought, a small dish holding a perfectly-sliced piece of cherry pie topped with a dollop of whipped cream slid in front of him. It could have been straight out of a magazine the way the cherries lined up and the red popped on the white glass dish.

"It looked like you needed this," the waitress explained as she slid into the open booth across from him.

He didn't know how to respond; she had caught him at a time where his mind was on work, but his cock was fully present and beginning to stir, entirely focused on her.

He looked at the piece of pie, then up to her beautiful face. She looked even more sweetly innocent than the girls of the past did as she was illuminated softly under these warm yellow lights of the 1950s diner.

"On the house." She smiled.

"Thank you," was all he could muster as a response. His eyes settled on her red and white polka dot scarf tied elegantly around her slender neck.

An awkward moment of silence passed between them as a red blush brightened her cheeks. She had noticed his eyes were focusing somewhere on the vicinity of her top, and mistaking it as him looking at her breasts, which she probably received a lot, he watched as the blush spread across the bridge of her nose. It was adorable, and brought his mind back into the present with a slight sense of ease from the hellish day.

"You and your buddy have been here a lot these past couple of weeks," she observed casually.

"Have we?" he asked stupidly. "We're working a case. I guess this is a good place to come to convene and talk shop." The fact that she had noticed him and Donahue in the diner before, but he had not seen her, made something inside him stir. Flattery? Perhaps.

"You're cops?" she asked.

"Detectives."

"What are you working on now?"

He grinned. "I can't tell you that."

"Why?" Her lips curled into a silly young grin. "Is it confidential?" She probed playfully. "If you tell me, will you have to kill me?"

He laughed, even though the word "kill" panged at his heart and memories for a brief moment. He could have done without that.

He had heard that line a thousand times before, but from her, with that innocent tone and twinkling young and naïve eyes, it sounded new again.

"No, no," he dismissed with the wave of his hand. "I just don't want to lose my shield."

"Well, we wouldn't want that." She picked up a fork from the table, removed the tip of the pie and spooned it into her mouth. Her lips were just as red and glossy as the cherries on the plate. She turned the fork over and ran her tongue along the back of it, cleaning the white whipped cream from the metal prongs.

He felt his cock stir again. It had already been enticed just by her beauty, but now he was fully engrossed in the young waitress as he watched her tongue trace along the back of the silver fork, and the look in her eyes reciprocated his interest.

***

Ellis pushed Holly up against the tile wall of the unisex bathroom. The black and white checkerboard tiles lined the four walls as well as the floor. With the bright white lights overhead glistening off of the shiny surfaces, it made the washroom glow and glisten like a stage. It felt surreal, but the energy between them grounded them back to the present as they embraced and ravaged each other hungrily.

Holly's red skirt fell to the floor in a circle of fabric around her feet, which were still clad with her era-appropriate high heels. The cloth resembled a puddle of blood on the glistening tile. Even with his pecker moments away from being buried in this young girl, Ellis could still not completely purge morbid thoughts created by his job completely from his mind.

She gracefully stepped out of the circle of red fabric around her feet and blindly kicked it aside as she continued to kiss him. His hands grabbed around her tiny waist and he lifted her up, placing her on the vanity. She wrapped her legs around him and pressed against the crotch of his pants. His cock was fully hard beneath his slacks, and having it pressed tightly against her panties made the blood throb and pulse even stronger.

Engulfing her lips with his, he pushed the fabric of her panties aside and plunged two fingers into her hot and moist pussy. She gasped into his mouth upon his unexpected yet welcomed entry. He worked his fingers in and out, occasionally taking them out to rub and massage her clit. They slid easily against the small mound of flesh as the juices from her dripping and more-than-willing hole coated his fingers as he worked her, encouraging moans and sighs from her parted ruby lips.

She hungrily thrusted her hips into his fingers, pushing herself away from the vanity, trying desperately to get him to reach further inside of her. He shoved them as deep as they could go, but they both knew they would never satisfy her, not the way his cock would, which awaited eagerly.

She moaned with every movement he made into her, again and again. He could feel her pussy walls constrict around him, hot and wet. She was so ripe inside. So soft, so delicate. He pounded her harder with his fingers, knowing she was ready to cum as her moans became higher with each and every thrust of his hand. He was ready to push her over the edge and bring her to climax at his hand.

"Wes," she sighed. "Oh God, Wes."

It had been forever since he had heard his name used in a sexual setting. Celeste always called him 'Detective,' and his prior encounters usually referred to him as 'Sir.' Something in the back of his mind stirred, a distant memory. Something he didn't want to acknowledge. Instead he tried to concentrate on her and her oncoming climax.

He buried his face into her neck, below her jawline, and grazed her skin with his tongue. She tasted sweet, like strawberries. It was not a natural taste on his tongue, and there was no doubt she had used a body balm that enticed the taste buds in hopes of such an encounter tonight. He wondered where else she had coated her skin with the mouthwatering balm.

In one quick, skilled movement he removed her red polka dot scarf from her neck and let it fall to the bathroom floor. He sank his teeth into the soft skin that the fabric once hid and his mouth literally watered as he bit down into her neck. It was coated in strawberries there as well. She yelped beneath his bite and it only encouraged him to dig his teeth in deeper as he stroked her clit.

She bucked beneath him, but his grasp was firm around her with his free hand. She dug her fingers into his hair and pulled. He had a flash of Celeste move through his mind's eye, but he knew this grip did not mean to imply Holly's action as one of control. It was merely a reaction to the pain, a reaction he was very familiar with—one that made his cock throb in anticipation.

Releasing his teeth from her, he wrapped his hand that was once holding her body now around her neck. He dug his fingers into the freshly sensitive area and deep bruising of where he'd just bitten, savoring the sounds of her squealing beneath him at the pain.

He brought his other hand that was pleasuring her to her face and guided his soaked fingers in to her mouth. She suckled on them hungrily as he worked them in and out, gliding along her soft tongue, slowly moving them further and further inside. She looked at him with her big, innocent eyes as his fingertips reached toward her throat, while his other hand stayed on her neck.

He grinned a sadistic grin, as he removed his fingers from her mouth to join his other hand around her neck. Gently he squeezed them around her windpipe, intently watching her eyes for a reaction. He loved experiencing that moment when passion changed, and how quickly it did. In a brief moment, as quick as the flutter of butterfly wings, it would become one of terror. Quietly he watched for it, his eyes locked on hers.

In his experience, he knew those first few seconds of realization were small, and almost unnoticeable to the untrained eye. Yet if you looked close enough, you could see the pupils begin to dilate, widening in their first realization that the lungs were out of air and they could no longer draw in another breath.

Next that glorious noise of their first attempt to breathe air into the lungs would follow. Almost right on cue she did so, and a sadistic smile spread on his lips. Her pupils were now wide, deep black puddles.

His experience told him if they opened their mouth to try and draw in air, you could hear their tongue click near the back of the throat, trying to bring in oxygen fruitlessly. Her chest would then tighten beneath her breasts, her lungs cued to go into a frenzied panic. When they began to strain and hurt, that is when the real dread would set in—that their breathing was no longer in their own control. This look of realization, mixed with apprehension and sometimes terror, would certainly be observed by even the most casual observer.

These clicking noises mixed with empty and shallow attempted breaths were what Holly was making now. The detective's hands didn't leave her throat, despite her silent protest in her eyes. They were starting to lose a little bit of light. She desperately gurgled and tried to bring in oxygen down her throat, but there was none to be had. Not until he let her, of course.

Her body then bucked and rebelled on the bathroom vanity she sat upon, and this is when he would always tighten his grip on his girls. Depending on the girl, they would either leave their eyes open in fear, which he enjoyed the most, or they would close their eyes, as Holly was doing now.

He couldn't have this, he wouldn't. It was the fear that turned him on and fed him. He brought his dominant hand against her cheek in a quick slap. She snapped open her eyes; they were startled and big.

"Keep your eyes open," he ordered, as he stroked the side of her face where he had just slapped.

He could see her skin beneath his caressing fingers begin to turn brighter and brighter by the moment as her oxygen-starved lungs must have been screaming beneath her perfect breasts. Soon her face was just as red as her skirt.

Finally he released her from his grasp, and she took in that first vital breath of air that felt like swallowing a solid object as she pulled it painfully into her lungs. It also probably felt like the sweetest and purest breath of air she had ever taken into her lungs, after being deprived for what had felt like a lifetime.

Her breasts heaved up and down as she took in those first long pulls of air. Her pupils returned to their normal size, and her cheeks now went from bright red to just a flushed pink. This would be the moment that defined her as a bottom. How would she react? Ellis considered himself a good judge of character, and he assumed her reaction when he ran the scenario through his mind, the first time he had set eyes on her, but people still occasionally surprised him—very occasionally.

She reached for Ellis to pull him back in to her, as he expected. He grinned to himself as he pressed his lips against hers. It was rare for a submissive not to be turned on by the adrenaline rush of nearly passing out, and now Holly's body was vibrating with it. She dug her fingernails into his back and her sounds became more intense and primal.

He grabbed a handful of her hair and pulled her head back, sinking his teeth back into that same spot as before. It had already bruised beneath the skin and was no doubt sensitive to the touch, so it was an optimal place to bite. The sound she made was the first real scream of their encounter, and it echoed off of the cold tile walls and back to his ears. He was finally ready to take her as he unlatched his belt when a pounding came from the bathroom door.

"Holly, break is over!" a female's voice called from the other side.

The young waitress rolled her eyes in frustration and sighed. She hopped off of the counter gracefully and began to collect her clothes from the floor. Ellis just stood there, his hard-on throbbing and unsatisfied, a look of disbelief on his face. She turned to see his expression and a small laugh escaped her lips.

"Sorry, Detective." She quickly kissed his lips as she zipped her skirt back on. "Duty calls," she jested playfully.

Holly took a blank ticket from her check pad, scrawled her name and phone number on it and tucked it into the detective's outside coat pocket. "Call me so we can finish this." She kissed his cheek and whispered in his ear. "Soon." With a wink, she turned on her high heels and was off and out of the bathroom to wait on a table just as if nothing had ever happened.

Ellis stood there for a moment, a little bewildered. Was he losing his touch?

This haunting feeling of being inadequate, not only at his job as the case went unsolved, but also the odd sense of emptiness he felt in his private life, haunted his thoughts his entire way home.

Chapter Fifteen

Receiving another early morning phone call about a deceased body was becoming all too normal for Ellis—too regular for comfort, and too common for him to want to close his eyes at night because he was afraid the next morning would bring with it another dead body.

He picked his clothes up off of the floor from the night before and slipped them back on, not bothering to look for something clean. He didn't shave, he skipped coffee, and the detective was out the door.

This time the vic was located not only in his part of town, but, as fate would have it, at the same diner he and Donahue had met at just days prior. The diner he'd eaten at last night. Ellis had a sinking feeling about this as he pulled up to the crime scene roped off by yellow crime tape. Donahue was already there, but the look on his face wasn't annoyance at his partner's tardiness, but rather compassion and and something else he couldn't put his finger on.

Before he could say a word as he entered beneath the crime tape, the greying detective laid eyes on the girl by the diner's dumpster. Her body was splayed out on the pavement haphazardly, as if she was trash, too heavy to be thrown away properly into the metal garbage receptacle. It was Holly.

She was still in her uniform from last night; the short red skirt adorned with a white poodle, a white keyhole blouse with an embroidered "H" on the upper left hand breast, and black high heels with red ankle socks.

However, studying her crumpled and discarded body now, he noticed one thing was missing—the red with white polka dot scarf that had been around her neck. The scarf he himself had taken off her in the bathroom just hours prior.

Her bare and exposed neck was covered in deep, fresh bruises. His bruises. His teeth marks. If Ellis's stomach wasn't empty, he would have vomited right there at the crime scene, much like he had in the medical examiner's office at the sight of Tina's missing eye.

He was sure the color had drained from his face, and he involuntarily loosened his tie from around his neck.

"I know, right?" Donahue said in response to his partner's physical reaction. "We just saw her alive three days ago."

Ellis was beyond thankful his reaction was misinterpreted by his partner for grief over an acquaintance. If Donahue was to know the truth, that he had seen Holly last night, he had no idea how he'd react, but he'd bet his last dollar it wouldn't be good.

Ellis looked at his feet, trying desperately to regulate his heartbeat and compose himself. That is when he noticed that the check Holly had slid into his pocket was making an appearance. It was sticking out of his breast pocket and exposing the first three digits of her phone number along with the "H" of her name. He quickly shoved it back down.

Donahue took the lead as he walked over to the dumpster. A cop quickly caught up on his heels to fill the detectives in on what they'd found upon their arrival, confirming they didn't touch anything. Ellis didn't hear any of it—his eyes were fixated on the young woman he'd nearly fucked less than twelve hours ago.

After being briefed by the officer, Donahue's eyes finally met Ellis, who was standing behind him looking down at the body of the waitress.

"You ok, Ellis?" he asked, breaking him from his thoughts. "You look like you've seen a ghost."

Ellis cleared his throat. "Actually, no. I woke up feeling like shit this morning. Must have been something I ate," he lied.

"Why don't you go home? I've got this."

"Yeah?"

"Yeah, swing by the precinct later and I'll bring you up to date."

Ellis nodded and, without another word, ducked back out under the crime scene tape.

He couldn't return home yet. He needed to breathe, get some fresh air. He felt as if someone had kicked him in the chest, breaking his ribs and depriving him from taking an adequate breath of air into his lungs without a heavy pain accompanying it. Images of Holly's body at the foot of the dumpster wouldn't leave his mind.

As he walked, he also played back the night before where he'd very nearly had Holly for himself. Her young, supple body, eager and willing. His sexual frustration and denial of release made his cock eager and ready to go at just the mere thought of fucking the young waitress in the bathroom, and his near miss. Even now his cock betrayed him as it stiffened beneath his pants.

It pulsated and pressed against the fabric, refusing to subside. He hadn't cum in what seemed like weeks, not since the night Celeste had left his bed made and his toys cleaned and organized. Ellis swore he could still detect the taste of strawberries on his lips from Holly.

His cock tightened. He thought of cumming in the young waitress and he found his hand rubbing the outside of his pants as he wandered the streets aimlessly. Fortunately there were no spectators, but just to be sure, he walked into a vacant alley, unable to ignore his erection any longer.

With a quick cursory glance around the alley, ensuring he was indeed alone, he removed his throbbing cock from his slacks and palmed it in his hand, stroking firmly.

A sigh of instant pleasure released from his lips as he closed his eyes, moving his hand along the shaft of his hardened penis, sliding the foreskin up and down over the pink head. He couldn't remember the last time he was this hard, and if he'd wanted to savor it and edge himself to a magnificent orgasm, he easily could have. However, that was not his intention this morning. All he wanted to do was cum, and cum hard.

The images of the asphyxiation scene he'd had with the waitress the prior night flashed through his head. He could hear her gasps before all of the air had left her lungs, and small, sick gurgling noises that came from her wet, open mouth. He remembered sticking his tongue into that hot mouth, embracing her in a kiss that was one-sided and primal, as she didn't have the capacity to kiss back while she struggled to breathe.

His hand worked feverishly along his cock, feeling pre-cum bead along the top of the head and moisten his hand, making his jerking motions smooth and warm.

Pulling away from the kiss, he looked into her eyes which silently screamed for air. He could tell she wasn't as seasoned at breath play as Celeste, and she would run out of air soon and pass out. However, something inside of him wanted to keep squeezing that perfect little neck of hers. So what if he left marks; that cute polka dot scarf would cover it at work tomorrow.

She began to claw at his hands that cut off her airway, moving up to his wrists and then forearms, trying to tug them away. Her effort was cute, but fruitless.

Leaning one hand against the side of the building, he supported his weight as he feverishly pulled and tugged at his cock, working the foreskin up and down, over and over again. As he quickened his pace, he could now feel the trembles of pre-orgasm pulsate through his cock.

Remembering her eyes, remembering when she'd mouthed the word "please," only made him work faster. A sweat had broken out along his forehead, and his cheeks became feverishly pink as rubbed his head to use the gathering semen and continue to slide his hand along his eager shaft.

Suddenly, images of the crime scene flashed in front of his closed eyes. The bruises on her neck, her bloodshot eyes, the cold emptiness of her pupils. However, his hand kept working. He was so close to climaxing, and his cock was rock hard in his palm. The scent of his pre-cum filled his nostrils and inched him closer to that moment.

He forced his mind back to the prior night, thinking of the desperation in her eyes, her face reddening from the oxygen deprivation. Another flash interrupted him, this time of the porcelain blue-tinted skin only the deceased wore. How her cheeks were no longer on fire with blood, but cold to the touch. He felt his cock throb, and the throngs of orgasm began to tighten his penis in his hand.

He struggled to keep his focus on the girl while she was alive. The crime scene was too damned fresh in his mind, and his detective brain couldn't turn off and separate the two experiences. At least, that's what he told himself.

Finally he released the girl from his grasp, leaving her gasping and panting for air. Her breasts heaved as she took in those first painful pulls of air into her oxygen deprived lungs. Remembering how her eyes came back from that glossy look that had glazed over them while his hand was wrapped around her neck, he finally felt himself let go, releasing his cum into the alleyway in white, thick streams as he let out a moan of success, relief, and exhaustion.

The white creamy substance splattered against the brick wall in front of him, and he continued to work his hand along his shaft until the streams lessened in quantity and finally even the drops he squeezed from his pink head came to a stop.

The euphoria seeped in, but instead of being able to ride out the feeling, it was immediately pushed away as guilt replaced the gratification of the climax he had just achieved. That was the hardest and most intense orgasm he had experienced at his own hand in a long time, and the last thing he wanted to do was question why, but his mind unwillingly went there.

Did he really just jerk off to a dead waitress who'd died from asphyxiation? No ... of course not. That was a line he would never cross. Sure, asphyxiation was his fetish, but he only got pleasure by delivering it to his consenting bottoms, not seeing it as a cause of death. He had seen it dozens of times in his line of work, and never once had he brought it home with him as spank bank material.

Surely he'd just had those images intermixed with his memories because the crime scene was so fresh in his mind. He would never become aroused by a dead body, and he knew that about himself. That was a line he would never cross, no matter the cause of death. No matter his own fetishes.

The only reason he'd become aroused at the crime scene is because it reminded him of the scenes he'd had with past submissives where he had choked them, consensually, and got off sexually afterwards.

However, there was always that voice in the back of Ellis's mind, that voice he couldn't shut up. Today it seemed louder and more validated due to being as sleep deprived as he currently was. The voice quickly made his stomach churn, his esophagus contract, and the bile from his stomach heave up into the alleyway, landing at his feet.

His body contradicted him as he tried desperately to rationalize his thoughts, and he felt sick. No, he *got* sick, what he *felt* was disgusting. What was wrong with him? He ran the back of his coat sleeve over his lips, spitting the vile taste out of his mouth.

Without thinking, he angrily flung out his balled-up fist and hit the brick wall in front of him to clear the voices with thought-shattering pain. Instantly the agony from the solid bricks broke his inner monologue's questioning, and it felt as if his knuckles exploded under the skin.

The skin containing the bones was instantly torn from the muscles, releasing a cascade of blood. It warmly flowed over the back of his hand and down his forearm. He clutched his arm painfully at the wrist, holding the bloody mess out in front of him and watching the crimson drops fall and hit the pavement, mixing with his fresh vomit.

"FUCK!" he screamed angrily, more at himself than at the pain.

He had broken bones before, and he was fortunate this wasn't the case this time, but it didn't change the fact that it still hurt like a bitch. He removed his handkerchief from his pocket and wrapped it around his bloody knuckles. The blood immediately seeped through the thin material and he knew he might need stitches. However, the possible hospital trip, the searing pain, and even the vomit at his feet were all much easier to accept and deal with than the images and thoughts that currently subsided into the recesses of his brain.

Chapter Sixteen

That night, Ellis sat in his darkened apartment nursing a bottle of whisky he had bought on his way home. His intention had been to go to the pharmacy to purchase supplies to bandage up his hand, but somehow, afterwards, he found himself wandering through the aisles of the liquor store next door. Regardless of how it happened, or even why, he now sat on his couch overpouring himself another glass of the amber-colored alcohol with his good hand.

His right hand was crudely bandaged in white gauze and tape. Blood seeped through the woven material, proclaiming each knuckle that he had ripped open on the brick wall. Whenever he flexed his hand to pick up the glass, he winced in pain, and the broken skin which was finally beginning to scab over was torn open again and new blood moistened the poor excuse for a bandage.

The bottle was already a third of the way empty, and Ellis was beyond incapacitated. Being sober for the past ten years made his tolerance shit, and he was far gone after the third shot, let alone a third of the bottle. Now his head swam with the prior night's events, followed by today's crime scene in a hazy fog of alcohol, guilt, and disgust.

What would they find on Holly during the autopsy? His own DNA in one form or another, no doubt. Epithelials from his hands around her neck. Probably fibers from his clothes and hair as well. Any baby-faced beat cop could have told you the basic principles of transference, which meant where there was some of him on her, there was some of her on him as well. Maybe if he was lucky, he could play it off by saying he had been a responding detective at the scene.

However, somewhere in the back of his mind he knew this would not fly, which is why he'd come home and showered. He'd scrubbed his skin raw under the scalding hot showerhead for an hour. The pumice stone he bought at the pharmacy with his medical supplies made his skin red and angry, but besides using bleach, he couldn't think of a better way to help separate himself from any physical evidence.

He also threw away the clothes and shoes from last night in a dumpster the next town over. Despite his innocence, he had to cover his tracks. He couldn't afford the connection; it was too suspicious. Yet no matter what he did, there was one element he couldn't erase or dispose of—the human element. There were witnesses who saw him with Holly the night she was murdered. He couldn't get rid of them, too. He drowned this thought in another glass of whisky.

Whether his actions to defer attention from himself were the right thing to do or not, the panic had set in. Nothing rational ever happens when that grasp of fear takes hold of your brain.

So now he sat here in the dark, nothing but the moonlight streaming in through the sliding glass door leading to his balcony. The liquor bottle in front of him and the glass in his damaged hand glinted and glistened in the darkened room. The only sound was the occasional crack of the ice cubes.

It had been nearly ten years since he'd had his last drink. Almost an entire decade. Yet now, with one weak moment brought on by irrational fear and guilt, he had washed that all away.

That first sip was easy, much easier than it should have been. He had now lapsed back into his old habits and his demons were released. With that first sip that had passed his lips and washed over his tongue, his past was free to haunt him once again. The chains of confinement where he stored his demons were broken, and he had only himself to blame.

The darkness of the adolescence he'd worked so hard to imprison in a deep, dark recess of his brain had escaped. On rare occasions, the dark images of his past had haunted his dreams when his defenses were immobilized by sleep. Other times, they would whisper in his ear every once in a while, just to remind him they were still there—he had not rid himself completely of them. However, now he knew that this time the demons were out for good. They'd been released to plague him without restraint, and he had learned a long time ago the only way to silence them was with alcohol. However, he questioned if this would even work now. Despite being three sheets to the wind as he sat in his darkened living room all alone, Ellis knew good and well he was in deep shit.

Chapter Seventeen

That night, Ellis sat in his usual corner of the bar he had frequented when he was a regular. He was surprised to find the bar was still there when he'd stumbled upon it this night, and even more surprised when the bartender had recognized him and recalled his drink.

While alcohol was a cornerstone of the past and had long since faded in importance, there were still bars to tend to those who needed a solitary or group activity that didn't involve kink. This was exactly what Ellis needed this evening.

Since Holly's death only a few days ago, there was not a moment when he hadn't been at some level of inebriation; he was just finding that some levels were higher functioning than others. Oddly enough, that "functioning alcoholic" façade was not something you lost even when you had gone dry. Ellis was currently learning how easy it was to fall back into old habits.

He remembered the days he used to visit and have just a soda or water amongst the crowded bar. He would test himself, if for no other reason than to just prove to himself that he could avoid alcohol. This is where he'd learned that his demons weren't destroyed by the alcohol, but were merely silenced by it. How he needed that silence now—but it had yet to deafen the noise inside his head.

Two empty shot glasses and a pitcher of beer, almost emptied, accompanied him at his table. For a Thursday evening, the bar was quiet. Only a few couples occupied the countertop, a group was scattered amongst the pool tables in back, and there was no one performing on the stage to the far right side.

It was a cold night on the hot town, and it was nearly eleven o'clock. He'd assumed it was about nine when he sat down, and many of the bar's patrons were either at home cuddling fireside or in dungeons making their own heat. How he longed for that passion as he sat there alone.

Tonight, his back was facing the door—he needed the solitude, and didn't want to be recognized by those on the force, or even acquaintances in the scene. However, it took him by surprise when the leggy blonde with a headful of loose golden curls and red lipstick sat across from him.

"Good evening, Detective," she purred. Even over the smell of freshly lit cigarettes and stench of old beer and liquor that had long settled into the wooden tabletop, he could still smell her naturally intoxicating scent. It went straight to his brain the way alcohol never could.

Tonight she wore a thigh-length white cotton trench coat that hugged her form perfectly. It was snow white and spotless, giving her complexion a soft, rosy glow in contrast to the fabric. Beneath the hemline, he could see Cuban stockings leading to red high heels. She sat on the edge of the booth, crossing her legs elegantly, one slender leg over the other.

"Celeste," he smiled. "I would never have expected to see you here." From the events of the prior days and the amount of alcohol in his system, he wasn't entirely sure if he was dreaming this encounter, or if it was actually unfolding right in front of him. His head whirled, coming to a stop on her delicate facial features and that half smile she gave whenever she was amused by something he said.

"And yet, I knew exactly where to find *you*," she mused as she reached her hand across the table and let two slender fingers find their way along his unshaven cheek and down to his strongly defined jawline. Her soft touch caused him to realize this was in fact real. Her fingers being so close to his nose filled him with the scent of her skin, and his cock immediately began to collect blood.

Her eyes went to the empty shot glasses in front of him, and then to his bandaged hand that lifted the mug of beer to his lips for another drink. Her red painted nail traced the rim of the empty shot glass and she looked back up to him. Concern crossed her eyes. She knew he was a recovering alcoholic, and this was not a good sign. However, she was not his mother, and she was not going to discipline him on his actions.

"How is your evening, Detective?" The way she said "detective" always made his blood boil. She never called him by his name, never "Sir" or "Master." In fact, when she used his professional title she purred it, making it sound like a title any Dominant would want to be addressed by, especially when the one saying it was as beautiful as Celeste.

"Could be better," he admitted, gently taking her hand with his injured one and kissing the back of it.

She let him kiss and caress the back of her hand for a moment before taking it back and standing up. She strolled over to him with her long legs and sat down on the hard booth next to him. One hand caressed his aging hair while the other rubbed against his thigh. She leaned into his ear and breathed softly as her lips found his grizzled cheek and kissed it with her satin lips.

She moved the nearly empty glass of beer away from him as she ran the fingers of her free hand through his hair. She slid it nonchalantly across the table. Ellis was so captivated by her presence that he didn't even notice.

"Do you want to make your night better?" she breathed softly into his ear.

***

The two stumbled into the bedroom, not bothering to turn on the lights. Ellis guided her backwards as she peeled out of her coat. The white garment hit the floor just before she collapsed onto the bed, his head cradling hers so she didn't hit it uncomfortably upon her landing. She looked up at him with her big blue eyes and grinned at his thoughtfulness, even in his drunken state, then leaned up and hungrily kissed his lips.

He kissed her back, taking her bottom lip in his and biting down until a small squeal escaped her lips into his mouth. God he loved the noises she made. He then moved down to her neck, hungrily biting and releasing her skin only to bite her again and again along the soft and recently untouched skin.

As he continued to bite and kiss along the vulnerable areas of her neck, he buried his face into her soft hair, breathing deeply. He then slowly made his way to her shoulder with his tongue.

She ran her hands along his back, clawing her nails down his skin as she thrust her pelvis up to meet him, wrapping her legs around him to hold herself closely against him. Her dress had shifted upwards during this movement, and he could feel the heat from her pussy radiating through her panties and against his already hardened cock.

He bit down into her shoulder and she released a sigh of ecstasy that was so deep and satisfying that he thought he might cum in his pants before they even started. She lowered her back onto the bed but kept her legs wrapped tightly around him. Guiding her hands back to his front, she ripped his shirt open down the middle, popping each of the buttons and sending them flying into the dark room.

He removed his belt and snapped it. She grinned, but before she could say anything, he placed the leather strap around her neck and tightened it, bringing her face close to his. A small gasp escaped her lips as her eyes grew wide.

"What was that?" he grinned, loosening it just enough to let her speak.

She managed a whisper from beneath the belt now pressing against her neck. "Harder, Detective."

Those two little words were all he needed to hear. He tightened the belt, constricting her airway, and kissed her hot mouth. Despite not being able to breathe, she kissed him back; her panties were wet beneath the touch of his free hand.

Finding her clit, he rubbed it gently in small circles and released the belt just enough so she could breathe out a sigh of pleasure, but before she could breathe back in, the strap once again tightened. He looked into her eyes. They didn't look scared—in fact, they looked hungry. They sparkled—enticed, passionate, and wanting more. *Craving* more. So much more.

He released the belt once again to let her breathe. They each loved their games of cat and mouse equally. She took that first vital breath in, but, before it could reach her lungs, he slapped his open hand against her face. This was no love tap—he had hit her pretty firmly. Probably harder than a warm-up should have been, but he knew his girl, and he knew how she played. His hand against her cheek forced the air back out of her lungs painfully. The wind had been cleanly knocked out of her.

She looked up at him with a grin. He slapped her harder. She laughed her wind-chime tinkling laughter. *Oh, this girl,* he thought to himself. *My pain slut.* Again he slapped her hard, but to his surprise, a small trickle of blood escaped her bottom lip.

He froze for a moment—his composure wasn't quite slipping, but he didn't know how she was going to react. He had never hit her that hard. He'd never hit anyone that hard. He felt himself sober up to a more alert realization that maybe he wasn't as in control of the situation as he thought he had been.

Celeste reached up to touch the blood with her fingertips. It was so quiet you could hear the kitchen faucet drip behind the closed bedroom door. He didn't realize he had stopped breathing, waiting for her reaction. He froze. In fact, the whole room seemed to have frozen for that moment in time as she examined the blood on her fingertips. She then tasted it upon her tongue. After a painstakingly long minute, that impish smile he knew so well returned to her lips.

She grabbed his hair and pulled his head back, and kissed him fully. He could taste the blood from her lip in their embrace as their tongues pressed against each other. She was still there—she hadn't run. She saw how dark he could be and she embraced him. In this moment, clear from the muddling of alcohol in his brain, he knew she was his.

Celeste ran her hand along his rock-hard cock beneath his pants. He was as hot as she was. Ellis shoved her dress up past her stomach and ripped off her delicate satin panties. Her high heels, thigh-highs, and garter belt remained intact as she writhed on the bed beneath him. He then pushed off his own jeans, revealing his more-than-willing cock and straddled over his pain slut for the night. Her neck was red with strap marks as he leaned down to run his tongue along them, tasting the saltiness of the perspiration which had collected along her skin.

He leaned back up and ran his fingers delicately along the marks, appreciating his work. She followed his lead and arched her head back, exposing the softness of her neck to his wandering fingertips. All you could hear was her soft and bated breath in the dimly lit bedroom as anticipation built between them.

He then felt one of her hands pump his erection, pulling down his foreskin, then rubbing the drops of pre-cum that had accumulated along the head. His dick stood firmly at attention to her touch. He easily could have let her take control for the night and lain effortlessly as she pleased him with her many skills, but that wasn't his way.

Instead he closed his hand around her throat, and her hand responded by clasping tightly around his thick shaft, gliding along it. He was hard and waiting. She gasped for air and felt more pre-cum gather. She rubbed the creamy texture beneath her fingertips and felt her own juices begin to flow, causing her to boil from the inside out.

He watched her eyes. In the beginning he'd told her she could never close them as he choked her, and from that moment on she never had. Ever.

Looking down, he saw her blue eyes grow wider with each passing beat of her heart. The organ was working in overdrive now, and he could almost hear it. Or was that the pulsating of his own eager heart filling his ears?

In the silence, there was no doubt her own pulsating blood was all she could hear, pumping, throbbing, and pounding, silently screaming for air. He imagined her heart was racing fast in a flutter, like butterfly wings.

A small tear trickled down the corner of her eye and rolled down her flushed cheek. He collected it with his tongue as he continued to squeeze her neck. This was without a doubt the longest he had ever deprived her of oxygen. He felt her body tense beneath him, her hand still stroking his cock. However, the longer he squeezed, the slower her hand became. He watched her face as it turned another shade of red brighter, and eventually she surrendered the task of jerking him off entirely.

Her hand moved from his cock to the hand that wouldn't let her breathe, and she grasped tightly at his wrist. It was no matter, all he had to do was stare into those eyes to stay rock hard.

Her legs released from his sides and another tear found its way down her opposite cheek. The longer she couldn't breathe, the less she blinked as her eyes remained fixated on him, and it was now starting to strain her beautiful eyes as they became wide and intensely focused on him. While most girls silently pleaded with him to let them breathe, her own pleas were for him to use her any way he wished.

Her hands now moved to her sides, fruitlessly grabbing for the bed sheets, twisting them in her small fists. Small gasps and gurgling noises escaped her open mouth, sounding nothing like words as some girls tried to do. Instead they sounded like desperate attempts to bring in air—exactly what they were. Soon they faded to nothing, but her mouth remained open, and this is when he ran his tongue along her lips to taunt the fact that nothing was getting inside that pretty mouth of hers without his permission.

Most likely her vision would soon begin to blur. First the sides would become fuzzy and unclear, then it would lead to the inevitable and sudden blackout, but she didn't resist him. He knew she could have hand signaled their code for "red" or even pushed him away. For a small girl, she was quite strong, and he was sure the adrenaline coursing through her blood made her even more so. But she didn't. She surrendered completely and fully to him in this moment. This one painfully long and mutually intoxicating moment.

His appetite for his blue-eyed girl grew with each passing second. He couldn't wait any longer. In one quick movement he released her neck and shoved his cock between her wet and yearning thighs.

Her gasp for air was mixed with the gasp she made from his sudden and unannounced entrance inside of her. The noise she made exploded into the quiet room, sending chills down his spine. It was a noise he had never heard before, a sound which very nearly made him lose his load right then and there as he pushed through the entrance and slid deep inside her.

Her gasps for air and moans of pleasure bounced off of the bedroom walls and echoed in his ears as he deeply thrust into her warm pussy. She wrapped her legs around his back, one of her heels digging sharply into his skin, but all he could feel was his pulsating cock rubbing and pushing further into her as this position let him explore deeply inside.

He kept his hand at her throat but no longer squeezed. She took his hand that rested there and plunged his three center fingers down her throat. He curled his pinky and thumb inward to give her the full length of his digits as they disappeared into her mouth. He worked them in and out slowly, timed with the movements of his cock entering and leaving her pussy.

Now and only now did her eyes close as she enjoyed the feeling of him riding her glistening body. Seeing this, he quickly withdrew his hand, strings of saliva coming out with his fingers that were just nearly swallowed as deep as his cock was, and slapped her hard against the side of her face.

She took a broken and unexpected gasp of air into her lungs from his sudden departure from her mouth. She coughed, gurgled a bit from the saliva that now collected in her mouth, and then swallowed painfully.

"Keep your eyes open," he growled.

She nodded, not shaken, but too far gone in ecstasy to put any words together. He leaned down and captured her mouth with his. Their tongues danced as his thrusts quickened and she now released her legs from around him and held one against each side of his torso as he pumped.

He sucked at her bottom lip, then bit down hard, squeezing blood from the cut he had made earlier. He pulled away, running a fingertip across it. That crooked smile that drove her crazy crossed his lips.

"Good girl," he muttered. A sweat had long broken out along his forehead, and now began to glisten on his back and chest, mirroring her own perspiration on her breasts and stomach beneath him.

Her cheeks were beyond flushed—they were now red-hot and signaled of her oncoming orgasm. He loved to watch that deepening red glow spread from her breasts up her neck and across her beautiful face as she neared climax. Her golden hair tangled around her delicate yet exhausted face.

Ellis quickened his thrusts into her, and her moans deepened as his cock tensed up in anticipation of the inevitable and oncoming climax. He focused hard not to let go. It wasn't every night he was able to fuck Celeste, and tonight he was going to make it last, even if that meant he had to ride her raw until he was good and ready to release his load into her.

As if on cue, he could feel her body begin to tremble and her back arch beneath him. He had brought her to climax so many times in the past, he knew her telltale cues well enough as if they were his own. If her cheeks hadn't already been fiery red from depriving her so long of oxygen, they would be now.

She fought hard to keep her eyes open as the climax began from deep inside and threatened to escape through her loins. Her moans changed from deep resonating sounds to high, anticipatory noises of delight. Now her own speed was starting to surpass his, rubbing and pushing his cock against that one spot that made her shudder and bring her so close to being pushed over the edge. This made make his cock ready to explode as well, as he felt her hole close tight around him and push and pulse against his dick. It took every bit of self-control he could muster to prevent himself from releasing inside of her.

She finally let go and her body released the tension it once held, slowing its place and relaxing. However, he was surprised by what followed, something was different than their usual fuck sessions. As her body bucked against his as she came and her screams of delight followed, she then collapsed onto the bed, breathing hard.

She didn't continue to move and push against him. Was it possible? Had he exhausted her already? Her youth and energy had always surpassed his, but this time he appeared to have outlasted her. The ego boost sent adrenaline pumping through his veins.

Given her exhaustion and apparently intense orgasm, he knew she would be extra sensitive to his hard cock now, as it continued to rub

against her clit and pound into her. She panted, looking up at him, asking with her eyes if he was close. His cold, dark blue eyes responded with a resounding "no," and that is when she knew this wasn't about him coming, it was about him dominating her. It was about conquering her, taking what he wanted from her, and having no regard for whether she had cum or not. This was something different inside of him, and it made her shudder, but it also excited her in a way she had never felt before.

Out of all of her partners, he was the only one with enough self-control over his cock to ride her this long and hard, making her feel it for days after. She arched her head back into the pillow and opened her mouth in a silent scream as Ellis felt another orgasm shudder through her body, and this time her responses were more guttural and animalistic, as she was moving past pure pleasure and into the territory between pleasure and pain—the type of pain that felt so good that you grit your teeth through the agony of it, but you know damn well that tomorrow you're going to be in agony when you piss. He grinned again, feeling his cock signaling that he was ready to cum.

"Do you have one more in you, girl?" he asked, his breath quick and hot against her face.

By now a full sweat had broken out along each of them, and she finally began to move with his body again. Slowly at first, but coming up to speed. Exhausted but willing.

The air hung heavy with the scent of sex and sweat, the sheets beneath them were soaked from their rigorous activity. "Yes, Detective," she whispered, then licked at her dry lips, re-moistening them from all of her panting.

She arched her neck and lifted her legs up; with a quick repositioning she placed each leg on his shoulder, allowing him to enter fully into her. He felt his balls lap against her soft ass. He then quickened his pace, feeling them swing more firmly against her. He felt his cock push inside of her deeply, hungry and determined to fill her with his cum, even if her pussy was screaming at this point for him to stop from his vigorous actions.

Her moans were now moving further into the pain territory, a pain only a masochist could fully appreciate. It was a sensation that was so painful that only an orgasm could justify them. Without his orgasm, the pain would be all for nothing.

Suddenly her once pleasurable moans turned into screams of

uncontrolled passion as her body began to let go and trembled, quaking beneath his, wave after wave. It was this sound that made him lose his own load and cum within her hot walls, strong and thick.

This pent-up load felt like it was long overdue. She had stopped before he had, and he continued to push against her until every last bit of his cum was taken in by her hot pussy. Finally he collapsed over her, beyond exhausted, both mentally and physically. It took all of his effort to push himself off of her and reposition himself at her side, drained and weary. The adrenaline slowly slipped away and left his muscles aching in its wake.

He reached down, plunging two fingers into her, feeling their juices mix and coat him fully. She cringed and yipped from the sudden touch, sensitive to everything and anything. He enjoyed her reaction, and he loved her embrace of the pain he inflicted upon her.

He then removed his fingers and placed them into her mouth where she sucked on them slowly and appreciatively. Normally he would have shoved them down inside her throat until she gagged. However this was different, this was so she could taste and fully treasure the accomplishment of their work together. He allowed her to savor the taste and fucked her mouth with his fingers at her own pace until she chose to withdraw them.

Their breathing patterns were deep and exhausted. Purely ragged. She looked over at him, her hair soaked with perspiration, as was his. Her cheeks were blazing hot and her mascara and eyeliner ran down her face, but her red lipstick had remained intact.

Even through the crimson makeup, he could see the darkened gathering of blood from where her lip had separated from his strike, and now that his eyes were adjusting to the low lights of the bedroom, he could also see the shadow of a bruise begin to form on her cheek.

It had been forever since he had just fucked. Unrestricted, unbridled, raw, passionate fucking. Usually they would play, and play hard. However tonight it was different; tonight it was about something else. Tonight it had been pure dominance in the most primal of senses where he'd taken what he wanted with no regrets and regards for her, and she'd chosen to yield under him.

Despite her wrecked appearance, he could see the satisfaction in her eyes. It wasn't a normal evening for her, either, as she was not one for fucking without a lead-up of pain and suffering, but she must have

sensed tonight was different as well. Maybe she'd sensed it from the moment she saw him in the bar sitting alone. Either way, tonight had been simply hedonism at its best, and it left both of them with a new sense of achievement and passion for the other that, until now, they had yet to experience together.

Chapter Eighteen

The next morning, Ellis rolled over in his bed to place an arm around his sleeping beauty, but all he found was an armful of blankets. He unwillingly opened his eyes, knowing he'd see the empty bed next to him and a note on the pillow. When he finally lifted his eyelids, that's exactly what he saw.

Through the blurred vision of his hangover and raging headache, he squinted and saw, on the pillow next to him, there was indeed a white note. It lay folded neatly atop the dried blood drops from her injured lip the night before and wrinkled bed linens. It was crisp and white, just like every other note she had ever left him, bearing his name in her delicate handwriting. It was the only time she had ever used his name.

He took the paper, already having a gist of what it would say. Before he opened it to read what it contained, he noticed his knuckles had been re-bandaged. *Did Celeste do that before she left?* He remembered the sex. He remembered the sex incredibly well, but after that it was a bit of a blur. He must have passed out. It was the first good night's sleep he'd had in a long time, and, to top it off, he hadn't had a single dream or nightmare.

He unfolded the piece of paper and read the words to himself.

Wes,
Only a man such as yourself could ever make me feel the things you do. You are a true Dominant, and you don't need the tools of the trade to prove it. Your actions, your words, and that look in your eye is enough. Until next time…

~ c

He read the words over and over again. This note was different from the others; it was more personal and it touched something within him. Had she indeed felt a shift in their dynamic the way he had? Was she hinting at something more?

He pushed the thoughts from his mind. There was no way Celeste would ever settle down and be his, nor anyone's. Not in this world anyway. It was wishful thinking at best.

However, he would be lying to himself if he said he hadn't secretly hoped she would still be there this morning. No more notes, no more quietly letting herself out, just him and her wrapped up together in his bed until they were ready to begin the day. Together.

Chapter Nineteen

Regardless that his day didn't begin as he wanted it to with the company of his golden-haired Celeste, he still had work to do. He had to follow up on the latest medical examiner's report in their string of homicide victims.

Much to Ellis's surprise, when he arrived at the check-in desk, the body of his latest victim wasn't in Jensen's exam room. The word "victim" felt heavy in his mind as he knew this girl, but to give her an identity was difficult when the case was still open and being worked.

"Good morning, Alyssa. You look lovely as always." He offered her the smile that he knew made women blush, and that is exactly how she responded as she tried to cover her rosy cheeks with her long platinum hair.

The two had a brief history, and while it hadn't ended poorly, it had ended prematurely. He'd seen much more potential in it—obviously more than she had, as she was the one who'd blown the whistle on it.

However, that didn't mean he didn't hope to rekindle something between them. He looked down at the paper to see which room he was going to, but Jensen wasn't listed next to Holly's name.

"Does Doc have the day off?" he asked the pretty secretary as he scrawled his name on the clipboard in front of him.

"No, he left early," she responded meekly, avoiding eye contact. She turned back to her computer, and it appeared to Ellis as if she was trying to busy herself. Was she trying to evade his questioning? There was a strange tension in the air between them, and he had no idea why.

"Your vic is with Doctor Oliver. He's in room—"

Before she could finish, Ellis grabbed his overcoat from the receptionist counter and stalked away to the elevator. "I know what room he's in," he muttered angrily.

Getting off of the elevator, Ellis was no less angry or annoyed. It was pretty much unheard of for a body that was part of an ongoing case to be transferred to a new M.E. It was important for the same set of eyes to examine each body as it came into the office, especially when they were assumed to be connected to the same killer. This way the doctor could make connections and draw conclusions in relation to the previous bodies that a new M.E. would have no knowledge of. Having two doctors working the same case was going to mean twice the legwork for Ellis.

On the way to Oliver's exam room, the annoyed detective had half a mind to barge into Jensen's office and demand an explanation. However, after seeing the old man's response to Tina Nolan's body, he had a pretty good idea why he didn't want any more bodies in connection to this killer. It was the first time he'd ever seen the medical examiner in a human light, shed from his degrees and white coat, and vulnerable.

Perhaps the old man was losing his nerve in his old age. Perhaps he was just tired of seeing the cut up cadavers day in and day out. One thing was for certain—their perp was escalating, and if Doc Jensen couldn't handle the modern day Jack the Ripper before he really got going, perhaps it *was* best for him to step down.

Ellis had a feeling this was not going to be the last victim, and if there were indeed more they were not going to get any more palatable for the old doc. While part of him burned with anger that he had to report to a new coroner, another part of Ellis pitied the man for needing to step down and hand this body off to someone new. It must have taken a hit to his pride, and even more so to his humanity.

As far as this Oliver character went, Ellis had had past dealings with him before. While he had a distaste for Jensen, Oliver was a whole new breed of prick that Ellis wished to have nothing to do with.

They were roughly the same age, as they'd been through school together. They'd had many of the same core classes in criminology and basic criminal justice. While Ellis had followed the detective route, Oliver had gone down the medical examiner path. However, before their paths split, there was quite a bit of bad blood.

Of course it was over a girl. Both men were highly dominant, and each had seen competition in the other even before the girl entered their peripheral. Academic achievement was their first competition, followed closely by how each conducted themselves in dungeons and clubs. As students, they'd tended to travel within the same circles, and their paths always crossed.

They'd been civil in such situations, but all of that had changed when Selene entered their lives. To Oliver, Selene was a trophy, another notch on his belt. Ellis could tell by the conversations he had overheard at social gatherings, and the way he hounded her. However, to Ellis she was something more. She was an opportunity—a potential student and partner to learn from, and in return to help grow.

Oliver was the last M.E. he wanted to work with on this case.

"Why is my body not with Jensen?" Ellis barked.

"He refused to take it."

"Refused?" The word sounded foreign; it was never in his vocabulary at the medical examiner's office. "What do you mean he refused? How can you refuse a body?! It's his job!"

The young examiner shrugged. "All I know is he did, and I'm backlogged by about two days, so your vic is going to have to remain on ice until I'm caught up."

"She's part of an ongoing investigation!" Ellis rebelled in anger.

The M.E. gestured to the bodies on the metal tables around his office, as well as the wall of doors containing more within the refrigerated unit. "Take a number, Detective."

Ellis could have easily bantered with the man, but he knew it would have been pointless. Instead, he just stalked out of the office. He was fuming from Oliver's blatant display of disrespect toward him, but, even more so, he was mad that Jensen had put him in this position by refusing to take his body in the first place.

As he passed the frosted glass window of Jensen's office, he heard a noise come from inside. The old man was actually in there! Ellis decided this day couldn't get any worse, and he pushed his way into the medical examiner's room to confront the old man, who was leaning over a body on the exam table.

His eyes met Ellis's and they went wide and surprised with shock. "Ellis, what are you doing in here?"

"I want to know why you didn't take my vic." He tried to keep his tone even and calm, but it was already starting to break into anger.

"I was overbooked." He dropped his medical instruments from his gloved hands that were covered in blood from the body in front of him. "I don't have time."

ensen backed away until he met the wall behind
er him.

c. Why didn't you take her? You have never turned
orought you. Ever."

quickly left the old man and he looked up at the detective,
detec   you must know…" He sighed. "Holly was my niece."

Instai. y, Ellis felt like a piece of shit as he watched the doctor's face drain of color and emotion. "The case you're working on is progressively getting more and more dangerous. You must have noticed this with each victim, Ellis. In my entire profession, I can count the number of serial crimes I've dealt with on one hand, but this one is different. Now it is personal. I don't want part of it anymore."

All Ellis could do was muster a nod. "I understand."

The doc didn't know what personal was. This was the second victim he'd known, and it was starting to no longer feel like a coincidence. However, he was a different man than the medical examiner before him—he couldn't turn tail and run. He had to solve these crimes if he was ever going to get any form of resolution. Yet there was nothing else left to say.

Chapter Twenty

It was a Saturday night. A week had passed without the discovery of another body, but the two men had worked this job long enough to know that wouldn't be the case for long. The detectives also knew that if they had any hope of catching their killer they would have to be in the same place at the same time before he killed again.

After hitting the streets, they learned of a pop-up club happening that Saturday night just blocks from where the first victim was found. They knew the time and location, and, fortunately enough, they could easily buy their way in through the doorman, and that is exactly how Ellis gained entry that night.

Ellis entered the club easily enough, precisely as he expected. Greasing the palm of the doorman with a hundred dollar bill was enough to slip in without any questions or hassle. He probably could have gotten by with a fifty, but he didn't want to risk it. If their killer was going to be inside, then he wanted to make sure he was there to catch him.

Inside the building, he was surprised at how quickly they'd been able to get the abandoned warehouse to resemble a dungeon. It was not unlike the ones he himself had attended in his past. While the ones he'd gone to were in the secondary tier, he did indeed see similarities, and almost felt as if he was back in attendance from those days when dungeons were part of his weekly schedule.

It had been too long since Ellis had attended a dungeon. It was the mark of becoming old. Usually at his age, people would primarily play at home and invite others over to partake in the festivities. However, in order for that to happen you needed to *have* friends, and this was a luxury the aging detective fell short on.

Inside the warehouse, lights had been brought in to illuminate the darkness of the broken and dilapidated building. Candles were lit by the dozens, maybe even hundreds, around the vast, open space for the areas the lights could not reach. With their warm yellow glow, they illuminated naked bodies participating in a variety of activities. Their skin appeared tanned and bronzed in the candlelight as they writhed and moved with their partners in their various scenes. It was seductive being in the presence of so many players. It was like an orchestra of sight and sound that all made his head feel light and almost swoon with their passion.

In one area a young woman was tied up to a St. Andrew's Cross and being flogged. Her Top was using two leather floggers and florentining her back. It was a beautiful fluid motion where the man holding the implements swung them easily wrist over wrist, almost like nunchucks swinging in the hands of a well-trained martial artist.

The wrists and ankles of his beautiful bottom were bound to the cross so she couldn't move as the floggers repeatedly hit their mark along the young and supple skin on her back. The candlelight flickered and danced from the wind being cast off from the rhythmic pattern of the floggers. He could hear their impact creating a soft beat along her back, quickly licking against her skin.

Ellis could see she was gritting her teeth, trying to repress the sounds that were so close to breaking from her lips. The enduring bottom pressed her body forward into the cross. *As if she could get away,* Ellis thought to himself, as he grinned watching the beautiful scene. Traditionally the toys were made out of leather, but in the glint of the light, Ellis could see these were strands of rubber. No wonder she was trying to escape her Top's lashing. Leather floggers offered a smooth and soft flogging, but rubber—rubber was cruel. How they must have stung like a bitch! It was a testament to this Top's bottom that she remained as silent as she did while they struck her over and over again.

All of this time, Ellis had been primarily watching the bottom's reactions. Now as his eyes shifted, he could see the pride in her Top's face as she remained silent and, arguably, still. Every time he swung the straps, they hit the same spot on the middle of her back with skilled precision, and each time her skin would glow brighter and more alive. It was a possibility he would break the skin before the night was over if he persisted.

As Ellis continued his walk along the cold concrete floor, he took in the sounds of the patrons. Men and women alike moaned in pleasure and groaned under physical pain, and some were in the throes of passion and ecstasy as they neared orgasm, whether they were being directly sexually stimulated or aroused by the pain itself.

Unlike some establishments, fucking was always allowed in the tertiary sector clubs. From a mere cursory glance, he counted at least six or seven couples engaging in various forms of sexual activity already, and the evening had just begun. There were so many things that captivated the small audience that began to gather around them. Whether they watched out of fascination and awe or were simply turned on by the unfolding scene before them, all watched respectfully in silence.

One scene in particular caught his eye, where a woman was fisting a gentleman. Her liberally lubricated arm was nearly elbow-deep into his anus.

From an outsider's viewpoint, it was almost comical to view. The man was much larger than his female counterpart, but perhaps this was fortunate for him because a petite woman meant a slender arm and small bones. She had dark chestnut brown hair in a pixie cut, which emphasized her nymph-like features. Her nose was small and her cheekbones were defined, her slender and beautiful face giving her an ethereal appearance.

Her blue eyes were intense yet calm, and they reflected the control she had in this situation. She was focused, and the light in her eyes expressed that she was enjoying every minute of the control she had over this man.

He, on the other hand, was very large. He was at least a foot taller than her, probably more. It was hard to tell, given that he was on all fours on a table top facing away from her. While he had some extra weight on him that gravity was not kind to in the position he was instructed to remain in on the table, he also had his fair share of muscle mass with his broad chest and shoulders. His body was just as hairless as his naturally bald head, which now glistened with perspiration in the light cast off by the candles around them.

Barbed wire tattoos circled his biceps which now trembled beneath him. His hard exterior was in complete juxtaposition to her elf-like nimbleness and beauty.

He was on all fours and in excruciating pleasure—Ellis could see the man's cock was rock hard and dripping with pre-cum. His Ma'am would occasionally reach over to stroke his well-endowed cock, other times she would gently grab his testicles. These actions would send her subject trembling. A look of determination, mixed with him nearing his breaking point, fluctuated constantly by the second on his face.

"Please let me cum, Mistress," he whimpered.

She slid her arm a few more inches inside of him, to the surprise of the crowd. Hushed gasps escaped the lips of some of the spectators, while others grinned widely. She stroked her free hand along his pulsating cock. "Not yet," she instructed calmly. She was cool and collected, the exact opposite of her bottom.

"Yes, Mistress," he responded, reluctantly yet obediently. He bit his trembling bottom lip and tried to remain composed. A sweat had long broken out along his skin and was now dripping off of his red face. Droplets of sweat fell from the tip of his nose onto the table he supported himself on.

The small crowd that had gathered around the two now began to grow. Whether awaiting the epic cum shot once she allowed him to release, or to see how much more of her arm he could take into his anus, this crowd was truly curious and intrigued. Some were probably hoping he would cum early just to incur a punishment at her hands.

Not feeling overly compelled to see how the scene ended, Ellis continued his walk around the perimeter, dodging glances and avoiding eye contact when he could. He was dressed in his leather boots, leather pants, and a solid black t-shirt which displayed the muscles rippling through his arms that were normally hidden by button-down shirts and suit jackets.

In this scene, he knew he would catch the eye of women and men alike. He was considered attractive by most standards, which was surprising in such a diverse society where what was considered attractive changed by the minute.

He didn't have piercings, tattoos, rainbow-colored hair, or body modifications. He wasn't Goth, he didn't dress extravagantly or carry a flogger at his side as others around him were doing now. His attraction boiled down to the natural good looks of an aging and dignified gentleman, married with his evident experience, understated pride, and level-headed confidence. He had seen so many men and women come into this scene overconfident and arrogant. They were eager to build a name for themselves based on what they *said*, not what they *did*. Ellis had learned at a very young age that you should let your actions speak for you. Your techniques and how you treat those you play with, whether you are a Top or a bottom, will speak volumes of you, and word traveled quickly in this community, whether it was to promote you or destroy you.

However, being the newcomer here also gave Ellis attention he did not want. He did not wish to stand out as he was on the job, but blending in as a newcomer was very difficult in the scene. Dungeons and clubs were like families, and someone who entered alone, uninvited, and who remained isolated, sent up red flags to the alpha males and females in the vicinity.

If he'd been in the primary sector, the members there would be merely curious since the paperwork one had to go through to merit an invite was extensive. However, with the easy accessibility of the clubs in the tertiary sector, they had their own ways of dealing with suspicious newcomers, and Ellis hoped he wouldn't have to deal with this tonight.

Continuing his walk along the warehouse, he took in the crowd. While playing didn't mix well with alcohol or other substances, because it dulled the senses of the bottom and the reaction times and coordination of the Top, as well as reasonable judgment from both participants, it seemed to be flowing freely here.

However, the scenes being conducted around him appeared to be fairly well controlled. While this wasn't an official club by any means, he could easily spot those who took it upon themselves to monitor the activities of the participants in the open space. Traditionally, these men and women were called 'Dungeon Monitors' or D.M .s, and they were volunteers who kept the safety and the peace of the scene in line. While never appointed or required in the tertiary tier at these pop-up clubs that had fast and loose organization, it was an important aspect to keep the safety of everyone in check. He easily counted a dozen or so who walked the perimeter and looked in on the scenes, and they were most likely the men and women who took it upon themselves to do just this.

A scream suddenly rang out from across the dungeon, and many of the assumed D.M.s took off in that direction, as well as a fair share of spectators. Ellis immediately joined the crowd to see where the commotion was coming from.

A crowd was gathered around the source, and he assertively pushed his way through, garnering dirty looks and angry remarks from those he elbowed and shouldered past. When he finally broke through and made his way successfully to the front, he saw the source of the outcries were from a young woman struggling and being taken down by her Top. He felt like an idiot. Did he really expect a crime to be committed here out in the open of a public dungeon?

Just then, as he glanced to take in the crowd of onlookers, a head of golden hair caught his peripheral attention. He turned just in time to see it duck into one of the doors leading to the unused parts of the warehouse.

A familiar chill went down his spine, but he couldn't place it. He had known lots of blondes in his years, but this one was different. Her frame, the way she moved, the volume and flow of her dark honey locks … something about her rang different, and this is when the demons of his past began whispering in his ear. He pushed them aside.

He made his way out of the crowd, which was just as difficult as making his way in since people were now gathering thickly to see the scene behind him. In fact, many of the onlookers were now over at this part of the club, and, once he had separated himself from the massive group, he saw there were far fewer people occupying the club than he'd initially expected.

Pushing through the door, he saw the woman in question leaving again, now going into a vacant stairwell. As the door closed behind him, the sounds of the dungeon were muffled and all he could hear was the sound his own feet on the concrete floor. He had no idea why this woman was so important for him to find; all he knew was he had to. His agenda as a detective took a backseat to this new goal.

He heard a door close upstairs and he quickly ascended the staircase. It had been a long time since the staircase had been used, and he could see small footprints lightly displacing the coating of dust and grime that had been deposited over the years. The footprints appeared to be high-heeled shoes, and they had taken the third floor door to exit the stairwell, so that is where his own feet took him as well.

Once the door closed behind him, he was thrown into the darkness of the third floor. It smelled of mildew and must, with an undertone of old machine grease and paper ink. He probably should have inquired what this building used to be before he'd set foot into it, but from the surroundings and lingering scents from the past, he assumed it was an old newspaper or magazine factory—a physical media that had long ago died with the transition to the internet.

His eyes still saw spots from being plunged into the darkened third floor. He could begin to make out shapes of abandoned desks and file cabinets, as well as structural pillars supporting the floor above them.

Suddenly a moan came from somewhere within the dark recesses of the third floor. It wasn't a moan of pleasure, or even pain rooted in pleasure, as he had heard downstairs. This spine-tingling sound was a moan of pure pain rooted in agony. As distracted as he had once been coming up the stairs, detective mode set in and his eyes scanned the open space before him. Instinctively he reached for his gun, forgetting it wasn't there. On the chance of being frisked at the door, he hadn't risked bringing his firearm or his shield.

He kept his back against the wall so no blind spots were available for him to be taken by surprise. Once the wall ran out and he couldn't find the source of the noise, he moved to a desk, pushing his back against it as he squatted down, taking a low vantage point to scan more of the room. He could barely see ten yards in front of him at a time. *Christ, I wish I had a flashlight.*

Another moan sounded from somewhere in the darkness, but it was much closer this time. Did that mean the killer was close as well? Ellis noted there were at least two other people up here, the victim and the assailant, and he was at an extreme disadvantage as he could see neither of them.

He moved from desk to desk, keeping low and fast as he advanced. It wasn't until his third or fourth move that he saw the figure of a body slouched down on the floor against a pillar. The sound of pain resonated from her, and he knew he had found his victim. Ellis scanned the area for any signs of the perpetrator, but he saw no one else. Even though his eyes were beginning to adjust to the darkness, he knew he was taking a huge risk in advancing to the girl to assist her as she laid wounded on the ground. However, what choice did he have? He would have to render himself vulnerable if he was to help her.

He ran to her side and crouched down to her level. What he saw was much, much worse than what he had expected. The young woman was another submissive from his past, but this is not what made his breath catch in his throat. It was the gash along her neck that made his heart turn to ice and momentarily stop beating in his chest.

"Selene." He breathed out, horrified.

The mortified detective scooped her up into his arms and held her, his back against the pillar and the wounded woman in his lap. She was covered in blood, and he could feel it seeping warmly through his shirt.

He saw that the source of the blood was coming from the ghastly wound opening the young woman's neck. His hands automatically found it without thinking, and he applied pressure to try and lessen the bleeding.

He heard the retreat of feet fleeing in the opposite direction from where he'd entered the third floor, and his detective instincts instructed him to follow, but, looking down at the young woman who was now cradled in his arms, how could he? He noted the sounds of these footfalls were not the high heels he had initially followed, but heavy boots making their escape in long strides. However, that observation was all he could make, and he refused to give chase as he held Selene close to him.

He felt another source of fresh blood seep through her dress from her side. From where it soaked into his shirt, he predicted she had been stabbed in the kidneys. She was quickly bleeding out.

Looking into her face, even in the dim light, he could see the blood was quickly draining and she was getting paler by the moment. Her eyes were focused on him, wide and afraid. The blood pouring from her neck scared him, and he was never one to feel fear.

She recognized him and tried to mouth his name, but no sound escaped her lips. He clasped his hands around her throat together, trying to stifle the bleeding through the pressure, but it was no use. The blood ran through his fingers. It was thick and hot against his cold hands, flowing like warm syrup between his fingers and down his forearms.

She once again tried to talk, but it came out as gurgles and sputters. With every effort she made he could feel fresh blood pump and flow from the wound in her neck and spill over him. Some even came up through her teeth and lips as her attempts at words failed. Now it was slowly dribbling in blood bubbles and droplets from her open mouth.

"Shhh...." He cooed gently as if he was talking to a small child. "Please, please don't speak." He could feel the tears welling up in him. "It's going to be ok. You're going to be fine." The lies tasted bitter and heavy on his tongue, like he had been sucking on a mouthful of copper pennies. She tried to gurgle out words again, but this attempt was even weaker than the last. Her blinks began to become elongated and, with each one he feared she wouldn't open her eyes again.

"Stay with me, Selene," he urged her. "You're a tough girl, you can do this. The ambulance will be here any minute." The taste of lies enveloped his entire mouth now and he wanted to spit the taste out onto the concrete floor just to be able to swallow freely, but he couldn't. He would have to live with his lies.

Looking into her eyes, he could literally see the light fading from them, and never had he been so scared. He had only seen light fade from someone's eyes once before, and it wasn't any easier to watch now. Her hand on his arm began to loosen, and, before he could respond, Selene had released him completely from her grasp. Almost simultaneously he saw her pupils dilate, dark and cold. He watched in horror as they became large, dark puddles of emptiness. When the light fully escaped her eyes, he was able to release a tear from his own. He wiped at it with his arm and unavoidably smeared her blood across his cheek.

Suddenly a team of men and women outfitted in police uniforms entered the third floor of the warehouse. He saw their flashlights strobe and cut beams of light through the darkness as they tried to take in the area and evaluate any threats.

"Over here!" Ellis called, but the life was drained out of his voice and his words just sounded defeated and empty. He pulled himself up to his feet just as the first flashlight hit him.

"Hands up!" called out he owner of the beam of light that rested on his chest. Ellis did not doubt that where the officer's flashlight was aimed his gun was pointed as well. Ellis already had his hands up over his head by the time he was ordered to do so by the young cop. The last thing he wanted was to be shot by a rookie cop with an itchy trigger finger.

"I'm a detective," he announced as the obviously shaken officers slowly made their way forward. He could hear their hesitant steps on the cold concrete floor. A few of them now had their flashlights resting at his feet where they exposed Selene's deceased body covered in blood, the same blood that the wandering circles of lights revealed on the detective's hands, arms, and face. Soft murmurs broke out amongst them and he felt the tension shift to nervous fear in the vast open space.

"Just keep your hands up, sir!" the same cop shouted.

If Ellis couldn't find a way to de-escalate this situation, it was going to end very poorly, mostly for him, and result in a mountain of paperwork for whichever cop shot him first. However, with the body of Selene still at his feet and her blood not having even dried on his hands yet, he couldn't think straight to verbally navigate himself out of this situation. Fortunately for him, what he heard next was his saving grace.

"Put your weapons down!" a voice ordered from the back of the pack. Donahue emerged through the crowd of young cops and put a hand on the gun of the officer who had been shouting orders at Ellis the entire time. "Christ's sake, put it down!" he barked. "He's one of us."

A look of embarrassment came over the rookie cop's face as he holstered his weapon. "Sorry, sir."

Donahue closed the gap between the cops and Ellis with the paramedics on his heels. They quickly leaned down to examine the girl while Donahue led Ellis off to the side of the growing commotion. Now that Ellis was no longer seen as a suspect, the tension in the room was cut considerably and the cops began to search the premises.

"How'd he get away?" Donahue asked angrily in a hushed tone.

"Back staircase," Ellis responded distantly. "He knew I was here, Bob. There's no other reason he would have left her like this."

"Like what?" Donahue glanced over his shoulder at Selene as the paramedics shook their head to the detective, indicating she was no longer alive.

"Alive," Ellis answered simply.

The paramedics were now zipping her into a body bag. He could hear the crackle of the radios worn by the cops and the order to clear out the warehouse and detain the club goers.

Something suddenly occurred to him. "How did you know I'd be here, Bob?"

"Really" His partner half grinned. "Working together this long and you don't think I'd anticipate you'd come here?" He just nodded, his head trying to process everything that had occurred over what seemed like hours.

"They're not going to find him in the building." Despite being in a fog of emotions and having an effective coping mechanism of apathy, Ellis had heard the radios and took in their dialogue. "He's gone," he said to no one in particular as he remained in his faraway state of mind.

He knew the woman he'd followed upstairs wasn't Selene, but who *was* she? Was she a club goer, an accomplice, or even real? She had so many similarities to the woman who haunted his dreams, maybe he was starting to crack.

Being sleep deprived and driven half-insane by the personal turn this case had taken, Ellis couldn't help but think maybe he *had* imagined her.

"Put out a checkpoint within a five-mile radius," Donahue ordered the cop who was in charge of this poorly executed Mickey Mouse operation. He quickly took the order and relayed it into the radio on his shoulder.

The blood was now beginning to dry on Ellis's skin; it was becoming cold and had begun to itch. He couldn't stop thinking about the light going out of Selene's eyes. How scared she'd looked, how alone she must have felt. Without being able to say a single word, she most likely had wondered why she had been chosen by this stranger to die, and why now? Her eyes had also questioned why Ellis was there, a man she hadn't seen in years. So many questions, and not one could materialize on her blood-coated lips as she'd desperately tried to speak before she took her last painful breath.

These were the same questions Ellis had, and the worst part was he didn't have the slightest idea how to answer any of them.

Chapter Twenty-One

Selene's Story

Ellis had met Selene when he was in his mid to late twenties and just finishing up at the police academy. She attended the local college and was halfway through obtaining her degree in Sociology. She had to be around twenty years old at the time. They tended to share the same friends, and their paths would cross every now and then—at bars, clubs, dungeons, even at the library.

There was always an attraction between the two of them, ever since their eyes had first met. At the time, she was studying social sciences and she wanted to make the world a better place. She was naïve, but she also had the biggest heart Ellis had ever known.

Over beer and bad wine, they would get into friendly debates about topics she was studying that would continue until late at night. She had a perspective that supported human rights and incorporated psychology. He, on the other hand, used his law enforcement background to defend his points of rationality and procedure. They would then stumble back to one of their places and have sex into the early hours of the morning.

Selene had limited experience in being a submissive, but confided in Ellis she wanted him to show her more. While she was a natural bottom, she was very shy. It was something Ellis wasn't sure he wanted to undertake.

At the time, he was consumed with his schooling at the academy, and he was spread thin amongst a few other play partners who weren't always subtle in demanding his attention. However, the innocence about her intrigued him. It was rare for someone to be so far along in life and not have a better sense of who they were in the fetish community.

Playing with others in a D/s setting was a lot like fucking; some people were more reserved with who they fucked, while others would fuck anyone who spoke to them. It all depended on the person. However, Selene was still figuring out where she fit in at this time, and Ellis saw an opportunity not just to help her, but to broaden his own skills as a Top and perhaps Dominant.

Up until this point, with the exception of Tina and one other girl, Ellis had kept his Topping purely physical and platonic. It was a boundary he had set for himself and made clear to everyone who had the potential of wanting to be close to him. It was often the reason none of his dynamics lasted, as most of the girls wanted more. Most wanted love, and that was something he could no longer give.

If his dynamics did not end because of this reason, they just fizzled out due to the pure nature of the ups and downs of a Dominant/submissive relationship—each had taken what they needed from their initial union, and there was nowhere else to go. No hurt feelings, no throwing of belongings, just a mutual understanding and a parting of the ways. However, while he saw no potential to love Selene, he certain did see the potential to help her grow as a bottom, and that intrigued him.

***

Since he had first put a pair of restraints on Selene in his small city apartment that he kept during his time at the academy, he had sensed something in her just beneath the surface that he had to bring out. The fact that she trusted him enough to let him help her made him feel like he owed it to her.

They would get together sometimes three or four times a week to progress her journey as a bottom. She was willing and open to learn not just the physical aspects, but the mindset of serving as well.

Many people in the scene began disillusioned, by thinking bondage was just about sex and domination, but that wasn't true. A bottom had just as much power as the Top, perhaps more so, depending on who you asked.

A bottom had the right to say "yes" or "no" when negotiating a play scene with a potential Top. They also had the power to accept or decline being a submissive for a Dominant. They also set the rules of what they were comfortable with and what they enjoyed, as well as the things that did not bring them pleasure or gratification.

A bottom and a submissive willingly surrendered themselves to their Top; this is not something they could be forced to give or have taken from them against their will. To give themselves freely was a gift—and one that should never be taken lightly by anyone in the scene. This is what Selene learned first from Ellis.

During their time together, she blossomed into a beautiful young woman who found a sense of empowerment that made her not only a successful bottom, but gave her the confidence she needed in herself in her non-bondage related areas of life.

Upon her graduation from college, she accepted a job hours away from where they met, and they parted amicably, yet Ellis would never forget the things he had learned from her, as she would carry the things he'd imparted on her.

Chapter Twenty-Two

With Doc Jensen no longer taking his victims, Ellis knew exactly where his body was going to be, and he really, really didn't want to go there.

Ellis didn't tell anyone he knew the victim. He desperately tried to keep himself distanced from Selene and not refer to her by her name in his mind. However, he knew that once the boys in blue started digging a connection would be found sooner or later; in fact it was going to be much sooner than Ellis had initially anticipated.

He didn't know why he let it slip his mind—shock perhaps—but Oliver would make the connection between Ellis and Selene instantaneously. She was, after all, the girl who left Oliver for Ellis at the University.

Ellis had hoped the years would have been enough time to distance himself from any ill will Oliver might have still harbored for him, but he'd learned from the coroner's gruff greeting the other day in his exam room that Oliver was not one to offer forgiveness or understanding.

The detective, who had appeared to age another five years overnight, pushed open the door to Oliver's exam room. Before he could even get both feet across the threshold, he was taken violently by the neck of his jacket and forced up against a wall by the doctor.

The look in Oliver's eyes was wild and feral, like an untamed animal. His teeth were clenched together and he pulled in quick breaths through his flared nostrils. Ellis had expected he would need to brace himself for a verbal onslaught, but he hadn't predicted a physical assault as well.

"Oliver—" he began, but was quickly cut off by the red-faced medical examiner.

"This is your fault!" He pointed an angry finger toward a covered exam table behind him. Over his shoulder, Ellis could see a body beneath a sheet. Even though the head was covered, he knew who it was.

"Don't think I haven't put the connection between you and Tina together as well! When Selene came in, I looked at the past victims on this case. Do you think it's just coincidence you knew two of them, Ellis?!"

Three, Ellis thought to himself. His mind flashed to Holly in the parking lot of the 1950s diner. *First there was Tina, then Holly... now Selene made three.*

Before Oliver could say any more, Donahue appeared through the door. His partner seemed to be coming to his rescue a lot these days. He must have thought Ellis was taking the day off and decided to come follow up on Sel— the victim.

"What the hell is going on in here?!" he barked.

Donahue tried to pry Oliver's fingers from his partner's throat. If Oliver had been a pit bull, he would have had Ellis by a death grip around his neck, and, like any prize-fighting pitty, he wouldn't have released him, not until long after he was dead. That was the kind of anger that coursed through Oliver's veins, much like the anger that Donahue was trying to diffuse, or at least restrain, in an attempt to keep him from lunging at his partner again.

"Do you want to be arrested, Doc?" Donahue asked toughly. "Don't think I won't do it. You just assaulted an officer of the law." He struggled to keep the grip he had on Oliver secure.

"Officer of the law," Oliver mocked and spat at Ellis's feet.

"If it wasn't for the extenuating circumstances, I'd cuff your ass right now," he growled.

Oliver's eyes moved back and forth from his prey, Ellis, to the floor. He was seriously conflicted in that moment—ready to sacrifice everything he worked for, including his medical license, just for one more minute of having his hands around the throat of the man he blamed for the death of the woman lying on the table behind him.

After what seemed like an eternity, he stopped struggling and sighed. "Fine," he conceded.

Oliver finally loosened his grip and stalked to his desk. He picked up a folder and threw it on the counter between the two men.

"There's your fucking report," he spat venomously. He pointed his finger back at Ellis. "I don't want to see you in here again. You have something you need about this case, you send him," he explained, gesturing to Donahue.

Neither of the men acknowledged his order.

"Let's go," Donahue said dryly as he picked up the folder and walked Ellis out of the M.E.'s room.

Once they were down the hall from the officers and at the elevators around the corner, Donahue blocked his partner's hand as he went to reach for the button to summon the lift.

"I will only ask you this once, Ellis. How many of the victims of this ongoing investigation have you known?"

Ellis was surprised at not only the question, but the tone in his partner's voice. Just five minutes ago, he'd been at his defense, but now he sounded downright accusatory. The first instinct he had was to lie, but if Oliver had made the connection between himself and Selene, then it would only be a matter of time before everyone else knew too.

"Three," he responded dryly, not meeting Donahue's eyes. "Tina, which you knew. Holly, who we both knew. Now Selene."

"Christ, Wes. When were you going to tell me? One is coincidence… two, yeah maybe… but three?"

Ellis brought a hand up to rub the back of his neck painfully. "I don't know, Bob… It's like…" He paused to reconsider how he was going to end the sentence. "It's like someone is targeting me specifically by murdering these girls."

Donahue was taken aback by the statement. "You cocky son of a bitch. This isn't about you."

"Then how do you explain it, Bob?"

"Look, Ellis," his partner sighed. "You fucked a lot of girls. We both know this. Do you really think there's a connection?"

"I don't know," Ellis admitted somberly. "It's like you said, it doesn't look good that I know three out of four of them."

Donahue thought for a long minute.

"I'm going to try and keep this under wraps for the time being, and don't you tell anyone, either. We are going to figure this out. You just better pray you don't know the next body that pops up." He hit the button to call for the elevator, and the action seemed to break the tension of their conversation. "In the meantime, why don't you take some vacation time? I can handle the case for a week or two by myself, and you look like you could use the break."

Ellis considered it for a moment as the elevator arrived and the doors opened in front of them. "I'll think about it."

While he was grateful his partner wasn't jumping to the conclusion of a malicious connection between him and the victims, Ellis had a sinking feeling that his condition of not knowing any of the future victims wouldn't be able to be met. There was a serial killer in their city, and he certainly wasn't done killing yet.

Chapter Twenty-Three

After considering his partner's suggestion of taking time off, as well as his self-admitted near breakdown, the department granted Ellis up to two weeks of paid vacation time. He was adamantly against it at first, but Donahue talked him into taking the time off. He said he would take point on the case and update him with any new information that came to light as it happened.

Ellis didn't enjoy the thought of leaving an ongoing case, but he had to admit he wasn't functioning to his utmost potential. Maybe some time away from the case, and even the city, for at least a few days was what he needed to refresh his perspective.

It was really Celeste who cemented the choice to accept the time away from the job. After a night of debauchery and passion, he let it slip out that he was thinking about the paid reprieve.

She was lying with her head on his chest as he stroked her golden hair and explained the situation. As he spoke, she looked up at him with those big blue eyes that could have talked any man into doing anything, especially him. She remained quiet until he was done and then propped herself up, wrapped in a silver satin bed sheet.

"I think you should do it."

He was surprised she had an opinion on the matter at all. So many times he would talk and she would dutifully listen, but rarely did she have anything to contribute. She would usually just stay cuddled up next to him, somewhere in that state where exhaustion mixed with after-sex bliss. Every now and then, she'd offer a few words or small noises that resembled agreement and acknowledgement, but usually he led as well as carried the topic as she enjoyed the afterglow. However, unlike most nights, tonight she was quite interested.

"I've seen what this case has done to you." Her voice held concern, the same concern her eyes mirrored now. "I didn't want to say anything, but I've been worried. You talk in your sleep, and I've noticed you have begun drinking again." She bit her full bottom lip, hesitant, looking away for a moment, then fixing her eyes back upon him. "I know it's not my place to say anything, but if I may… I think this would be a good opportunity for you to catch your breath. Sort of recalibrate your brain."

Maybe it was because of the euphoria of the sex they had just had, or maybe it was due to the endorphins that were still firing in his brain after playing with her with the many toys that were now scattered around the room, but he agreed. Furthermore, he invited her to spend some of that time with him, and she accepted.

Celeste claimed it had been forever since she had left the city, and some fresh air sounded like exactly what she needed—what they both needed. Not to mention, the time they would spend together seemed long overdue, since their paths had crossed so rarely these past couple of months as the ongoing case dominated his life.

There was also something else that this trip brought with it— opportunity. The two had never shared a trip together, and perhaps those feelings that were lingering in him which had been amplified during their hedonistic night of pleasure weeks ago were reciprocated in her.

***

That is how he ended up here, at a secluded cottage on the outskirts of the city—a place where traffic noises ceased and the scent of the concrete jungle was replaced with the salty ocean air.

The small beach community four hours north of the city thrived during the summer, but it was after Labor Day, which meant the families that commonly occupied these cottages, hotels, and beach bungalows lining the shore were now back in their suburban neighborhoods. Summer vacation had come to a close and school was in session, leaving this community a ghost town and the peninsula deserted and desolate; this is exactly what Ellis needed.

The place he had rented was a two-bedroom, two-bath cottage with a large deck that wrapped around most of the one-story abode and overlooked the beach in the backyard. It was reminiscent of the houses you'd see in Cape Cod, and the weathering on the outside from the salty winds and rough winter swells added to its rural charm. Celeste fell in love with it as soon as they got out of the car.

Inside, the dark wood floorboards were all stained and had been shined to a mirror finish. The rafters were exposed at the high ceiling, and there was a stone fireplace in the living room as well as each of the bedrooms.

As Ellis looked beyond the large glass picture windows leading to the water, he could see Celeste sitting in one of the two Adirondack chairs in the sand. The back doors of the house opened right onto the beach, and there was no restraining the blonde-haired beauty from running outside to put her feet in the sand, no matter how chilly it was in the water.

In front of her, the ocean was lapping gently at the sugar-sand beach, and just to her right, a couple dozen yards away, was the dock leading into the ocean. Despite it being late in the season and the water chilly, he was sure she would try and get him to go skinny dipping. He suddenly saw the appeal of the multiple fireplaces.

The sun was starting to go down, and dusk was settling in for the evening. Ellis found the light switch leading to the back, and flipped it on to give his blue-eyed girl some light. Unexpectedly, hundreds of twinkling lights came to life in the trees and in the planters scattered around the porch. She turned, surprised, and he could see her eyes come to life as they reflected the fairy lights in awe. A genuine and childlike whimsical smile lit up her face and it made something inside his chest ache.

That ache was something he had been feeling more often than not lately, especially in her company. At first he tried not to acknowledge it, but you can only lie to yourself for so long. If he had been younger, if life was different, if his *past* had been different, he could possibly see this girl being the one for him. His primary, his girlfriend, perhaps even his wife one day. However that was a future that could never be, and he hated himself for it.

She walked back to the house, slipping through the glass sliding door and closing it quickly behind her, but not before a cool breeze followed her inside and rustled her golden locks, which she had ironed into loose, wavy curls today.

She wrapped her arms around Ellis and nuzzled against his chest, her cool skin pressed against his warm body. He held her in his arms as she placed her cheek against his sweater-clad chest. He was so much taller than her that she only came up to just below his neck, a perfect height for him to rest his chin on her head. He breathed in the scent of her hair—it smelled like ocean air mixed with strawberries.

If only things could have been different, he thought to himself once again, his heart aching beneath her cheek.

Chapter Twenty-Four

The next morning, Ellis awoke to the scent of coffee and bacon wafting into the bedroom from the kitchen. His head spun from the alcohol that still resonated through his system. He was still a little drunk, and when his bare feet hit the floor he had to steady himself.

Pulling on a pair of pajama pants, he followed his nose. Celeste stood in the kitchen wearing his button-down from the night prior. It was adorably large on her, covering her completely and draping down to just above her knees. She'd had to roll the sleeves up to be able to function properly around the kitchen, or else they would have undoubtedly covered her hands as she attempted to work. Her hair was a beautiful messy mane of loose curls.

He sat at the breakfast nook with an amused smile on his face. This was a new side of her he had never seen before. She smiled her morning greeting at him as she attended to a frying pan of eggs on the electric stovetop.

"I hope scrambled is ok. It's all I can do." She laughed her tinkling laughter.

"Scrambled is fine."

"Good. Coffee is ready if you want to pour yourself a cup." She gestured to the coffee pot behind her.

He wasn't sure if that was a jab at the fact she could still smell alcohol on his breath, or just her being courteous. Either way, he didn't let the fact that she didn't have a cup ready for him upon his entrance to the kitchen escape him. That was another one of those red flags he kept a mental tally of that made him wonder about her pure submissiveness. Yet there was no reason to start the morning off on the wrong foot, and he fixed himself a cup as she continued to prepare the bacon that sizzled on the burner next to the eggs. There was nothing in the world that made him hungrier than a good night of sex, bondage, and alcohol.

"They left this place pretty well stocked," she explained as she cooked.

He sipped on his black coffee and watched her work as she chatted. He grabbed a piece of toast she had browned and buttered generously.

"We should have enough food for lunch and dinner as well, if you don't want to go out."

The fact that he was watching Celeste cook breakfast was mind-blowing enough, but for her to offer to cook *more*—he couldn't believe it. He was witnessing a purely vanilla act by the kinkiest girl he had known, and it was ... well, it was endearing.

She felt him watching him and she turned, blushing.

"What?" she inquired, bashful.

"Nothing." He smiled stupidly. He felt that familiar ache again. If he could never experience her being his, then he would always have this moment. He stood up and sauntered over to her, then wrapped his arms around her from behind. "Thank you for coming with me," he whispered in her ear, and kissed the side of her neck.

"It's my pleasure, Detective." She picked up his hand that held her slender waist and kissed the back of it where his knuckles were not yet healed.

Ellis sighed quietly into her hair with his dark blue eyes closed, deep in thought. *God, this almost feels normal.*

***

After breakfast they spent the majority of the day exploring the beach, never seeing another living soul for the entirety of their activities. Even if they did, he was sure it wasn't unusual for people to fuck on the sand, as they did that afternoon.

He was right; Celeste did try to talk him into going into the ocean. After much adorable pleading, she settled for him pulling up his pantlegs and going in up to his shins. She was braver and ventured up to her thighs as she held her flowered skirt high around her waist, exposing her frost-blue satin panties. She squealed with delight and shock as it was indeed cold. However, the Indian summer sun kept them warm enough on the sand during the afternoon hours when it was high in the sky above them.

By the time they went back into the house, the sun was setting. He took his lovely little golden-haired beach bunny into the bedroom by her hand and laid her down onto the bed. He peeled her out of her clothes and wrapped her in the puffy cotton comforter to warm her up before fixing a fire.

He turned back to her and removed his shirt. He could feel the warmth of the fire on his back as he approached her and crawled onto the bed to embrace her with his lips. She tasted of the ocean, and her skin still held a slight chill. He took a handful of loose curls and pulled her out of the bed, standing her at the side, facing it.

He pulled her blouse over the top of her head, followed by taking down her skirt and panties. He leaned her over the mattress and ran his hands along her smooth ass. Slowly, he traveled down the back of her thighs and further down her legs, soft beneath his hands.

He breathed in her scent and he felt his cock become hard. He removed his pants and underwear, pressing his cock against her ass where her perfectly rounded cheeks met, then ran his hands over her back. As she stayed bent over, he pressed himself closer against her and used his nails to rake down along her spine.

She pressed herself against him, embracing the feel of his stiff cock against her round bottom. He pulled away and rubbed her ass again appreciatively with his hand and then brought it down across her backside in an open handed slap that cracked loudly. Her body moved forward on the bed with the force of it but she remained in position. He spanked her again, and he watched her body propel forward from the force.

A giggle escaped her lips and a proud smile crossed his. He spanked her again and again until a nice red glow spread across the skin he was working over and her giggles turned to yips and then moans of pleasure. He placed his fingers between her legs and felt she was wet from the attention.

He rubbed his hand against her bottom again and felt the heat radiate against his palm. His own cock was ready to take her from the spanking session. He found the bottle of lubricant on the nightstand and poured a generous amount into his open palm, coating his cock and palming his erection to feel it throb in his hand. He gave it a few good strokes. It wasn't going to go soft anytime soon.

He rubbed the lube between his fingers and coating them liberally, then danced his fingertips along the entrance of her ass as she continued to lean over the bed. He could hear her breath soft and waiting—waiting for his touch, waiting for his body to command hers.

Slowly he traced her pink hole, clean of hair and waiting to suck him inside. He gently entered a finger, and instantly she sighed at the delectable sensation. He worked it in and out, coating her with lube. Feeling the muscle tighten and relax in relation to his movement in and out made pre-cum gather along his throbbing cock.

He slipped another finger inside and a louder sigh released from her hot, moist lips. She moved herself gently with his motions, forward and backwards, craving him deeper than his fingers would reach, but not his cock. She made small little whimpers, whimpers that meant she wanted more, she wanted him. Ellis knew from past experiences she would cum from him fingering her ass if he continued to much longer. Grabbing her hips, he parted her legs and guided his cock into her from behind. She gasped deeply as he entered into her ass, and he pulled her back against him so her ass cheeks kissed against his thighs.

He smoothly slid in and out of her, in a slow rhythmic motion so she could feel every inch of him slip in and out. She moaned deeply and he felt her legs quiver. He loved the feel of her ass against him as he moved her into his motion, knowing his cock couldn't go any further, but that did not mean he couldn't try. Slowly he picked up speed. She moaned and writhed against the bed as she kept her body bent over the mattress. With the force of his cock exploring her ass she felt an orgasm quiver and begin to mount.

Celeste moved a hand to between her legs and played with herself, feeling her juices coat her fingers before she let them explore her pussy. Juices ran down her thigh as she heard him grunt from behind. He took a fistful of her hair and sharply pulled her head backwards making her yelp in pain. It brought her right to the edge of orgasm.

"Only your clit," he whispered into her ear, which was now so close to him as he clutched her hair. His message was short, but she knew it meant he didn't want her fingers inside of herself.

"Yes, Detective," she whispered, almost breathless.

"Good girl." He released her golden locks and pulled her hips back into him, repeatedly feeling her tight ass squeeze and move along his hard cock, pulling the foreskin back and begging him to release himself into her.

"Yes, Detective." She followed his order and obeyed and worked her fingers along the area she was allowed to.

As he pushed and thrusted her moans turned into screams of pleasure. A sweat had broken out along his forehead, and his body was warm from the heat of the fireplace. He placed a hand around her neck from behind and pulled her back against him as he continued to pump.

"Yes, yes, please..." she whispered with the little air he allowed her to have. She wanted to say more, beg more, but it came out gurgled and inaudible.

He loved when she was reduced to single monosyllabic words and eventually the animalistic grunts, moans, and even the occasional growl she made through gritted teeth as she was doing now. He felt the cum release from him in pulsating streams as he kept her body tightly against his and he filled her fully. Finally, when he was done, he released her and she slumped over onto the bed, weak, soaked, and spent.

He gingerly picked her up and set her onto the sheets, then took his position next to her. Her body was glistening and hot in the glow of the fire, and he gently wiped his finger against the beads of sweat that had gathered on her forehead, then across her cheek. Her eyes were closed from exhaustion but regardless she smiled weakly, exhausted and happy.

He quietly and reassuringly cooed a "shhh" in her ear, relaxing her. He placed a hand on her chest, feeling her heart flutter beneath as her lungs worked in overtime as his was doing now.

Finally her eyes began to flutter open, slowly at first as the fire's light was harsh compared to the darkness behind her lids. He gently shielded her eyes with his cupped hand as he smiled warmly, looking into her blue eyes and seeing the same emotions he felt mirrored in them. They didn't need to speak, and neither of them had the energy to. Instead he wrapped her in his arms and they quickly fell asleep to the sound of the ocean waves crashing outside.

***

Ellis woke sometime the next morning before sunrise to the sound of the shower. As he entered the bathroom, Celeste was just getting out. He noticed her ass cheeks were beginning to already bruise from his spanking earlier, and he was pleased with his work. He had caught her admiring it as well in the mirror before she noticed his presence in the doorway.

"Are you hungry?" she asked as she began to dry herself with a towel.

"Starving."

"Do you want me to make us something?"

"Why don't I go out and see what I can find," he suggested.

"Do you want me to come?"

"Again?" he teased, referring to her multiple orgasms the night before.

She blushed. He couldn't remember a time when he had made her blush, and it gave him a warm, satisfied feeling.

"You know what I mean," she giggled.

"No, stay here. Crawl into bed for a little while longer and enjoy the fire. I'll wake you up when I get back."

She was putting on a black satin chemise now. It hugged her body perfectly and he could see her hardened nipples beneath the fabric. He was ready to take her again, but that would have to wait.

"Ok," she agreed easily and gave him a long kiss on his lips. "I'll see you soon."

Chapter Twenty-Five

After an uneventful hour-long tour around the city trying to find an early morning breakfast joint, Ellis had come up empty-handed. He would have to try and replicate Celeste's cooking skills the morning prior if he wanted to give her the morning off from serving him, which he did. It was a strange feeling, a feeling he hadn't felt for anyone before. He wanted to please her.

However, that wasn't going to happen this morning. As he pulled the car around the corner to the street their beach cottage sat on, he saw a swarm of cop cars pulled up to the house. A sinking feeling hit in his stomach, and he knew something horrible had happened.

Ellis jumped out of the car without even turning it off. He elbowed his way past the cops and the yellow crime tape, despite their shouts and physical attempts at restraining him. He ducked around arms and out of the grasp of their hands. He pushed his way into the cottage, and he could instantly see through the living room onto the back porch where a female form laid, face positioned away toward the ocean, a mop of shockingly golden hair glistening in the sunlight.

She was wearing a black satin chemise, much like the one he'd seen Celeste in, just an hour or so before. But that couldn't be her... that couldn't be his girl.

Suddenly Donahue appeared, breaking his line of vision to the back of the house. Ellis could no longer see outside of the large picture windows.

"Wes..." he began.

Ellis couldn't read Donahue's facial expression, but something in his eyes reminded him of the way he looked when he'd arrived at the crime scene where they had found Holly, but it went even deeper into his expression.

"Wes, it's not good," he said in a low voice as he walked up to him.

Fear struck Ellis's body and he froze, every hair stood up on end. "What is it?"

Donahue took a breath in. "It's Celeste."

Ellis didn't think he heard him right. He must have asked him to repeat himself because Donahue placed both hands on his partner's shoulders firmly.

"It's Celeste, Wes."

"No, it can't be." He heard himself say the words, but he wasn't in control of them. The words repeated in his head, and it felt as if the wind was knocked out of him. "Let me see!"

He began to push past his partner, but Donahue held him firmly in place. His once comforting touch now restrained him.

Smart man, Ellis thought to himself. It was a technique he himself had used many times before when delivering bad news on the job. You don't know how a person is going to react when you tell them this kind of information, so you established a comforting hold on them to appear nonthreatening and supportive. If they wanted to push past you, then you could stop them; if they wanted to hit you then you could restrain them; and if they were going to faint, you could catch them.

However, none of that mattered now. All of his grief counseling and rationalization had gone out the window, and he became frantic, trying to get out of Donahue's grasp just like so many family members of murder victims before him that he had held the same exact way over the years.

Ellis struggled adamantly and was only able to see over his partner's shoulder for just a moment, catching a glimpse of the pale, petite body with a wave of shockingly golden blonde hair blowing in the breeze off of the water. The medical examiners from the county, strangers to Ellis and Donahue, were now zipping her into a black body bag. As they moved her shoulders to position her better inside of the bag, her head rolled to the side to face him.

In the morning sunlight glistening off of the ocean, he could see it was indeed his golden-haired beauty. His pain slut. His blue-eyed girl. However, something was different than when he saw her last—the sun was not catching the golden necklace bearing her lower-case "c," because it was not around her neck.

There was something else as well. In the early morning light, her closed eyelids glistened and sparkled. They were painted in Blue Morpho pigments.

wn!" Donahue ordered firmly, but with as much
uld muster for his partner while still trying to remain
keep him from entering the crime scene. "There's nothing
ao for her!"

No! I _need_ to see her."

"Stop, Wes, stop! I can't do that!" he ordered, in a tone that made Ellis finally cease and look at him.

"What? Why?"

Upon stopping his struggle against his partner, Ellis began to feel the adrenaline fade from his muscles and abandon his body, leaving him in a weakened and drained state. He looked up at his partner with confused and desperate eyes. "Why? Why can't I see her?"

Donahue sighed, trying to find the words, his grip still tight on him even though the tension had left his face. "They found your evidence on her, Wes."

"Of course they found my DNA on her, we were spending the weekend together!"

"It's worse than that." His partner seemed to be searching for the words. "There's evidence of foul play in the house." He let the words linger for a moment before he continued, but he could only get one word out before he had to stop again. "And—"

He paused for a moment, his eyes not meeting Ellis. Obviously this was hard for him, too. Ellis had brought Celeste over to his home on several occasions when they had dinner together with his family, or other times when the two couples had gone out on double dates.

"She was killed like the others, Wes. Strangulation and trauma around the neck." He let the words sink in before he continued, lowering his voice even more. Ellis had to struggle to hear him over the ocean wind. "Once the department found out a cop was renting the beach house, they called our department. I've been instructed to take you in as a suspect."

Killed. The word hung suspended in Ellis's mind. _Celeste. Killed. Strangulation._ These words playing over and over in his head did not sound right in whichever order he put them. This couldn't have been happening. This was supposed to be their weekend away. His time away from the case. His time away from the city, the crime. They were supposed to be safe here. Most of all, he was supposed to keep Celeste safe.

The expression in the detective's face must have said it all, because Donahue nodded in silent agreement.

"I know, it's crazy, but I have to. You aren't under arrest, I was able to talk them out of that, but you are going to be detained for questioning."

"I didn't do this, Bobby," he whispered in a broken voice.

"There was someone on the beach last night walking their dog. They said they heard a man and a woman fighting inside."

Ellis scanned the crowd and saw a man in a jogging suit talking to the officers. That must have been who Donahue was talking about, because when the man made eye contact with Ellis he immediately dropped his stare to the ground.

"Bob, when have you known Celeste and I ever to fight? For Christ's sake, we weren't fighting, we were fucking! I went out later this morning to find breakfast, but everything in the town was closed."

"Please, Wes, don't make a scene for the cameras. Don't make me cuff you. We can walk out of here, just you and me, and drive back to the station. Together." The tone of his voice was on the edge of pleading for his partner's cooperation. "Please, don't make this harder than it already is."

Ellis just looked at the ground and nodded his head silently. He looked over his partner's shoulder one last time to see the body bag was fully zipped and being loaded onto a stretcher. His head was void of emotions and thoughts as he let Donahue lead him to the car that was waiting take them back to the city.

"We don't know. Her body hasn't been found yet," Donahue explained, letting that sink in for a moment before he continued on. "With the exception of two girls, they can all be connected to you, Wes. Five out of seven, and something tells me if they dig, they are going to find a connection between Yvonne and Isabelle too."

"Isabelle?" The name of this victim was new to Ellis.

Donahue nodded as he removed a couple of papers from the folder he had carried in that was now on the desk. "She was found while you were out of the city."

He threw them down in front of Ellis. They were autopsy pictures of a young woman with the same cause of death as the rest of the girls—strangulation, this time manual. The expression on Ellis's face said it all.

"Fuck, Wes, her too?!" With disgust on his face, Donahue got up and walked away from the table, leaving the pictures where they laid. He faced the door, trying to collect and organize his thoughts. Ellis could sense the internal battle going on in his head, even without him facing his partner-turned-suspect.

It was most likely his ears playing tricks on him, the sleep deprivation setting in, the guilt from Celeste's death, the dehydration, or a combination of all of the above, but Ellis could have sworn he heard a gasp coming from behind the viewing mirror.

"No!" he shot back, but then immediately took it back since his past did indeed include an Isabelle. *That* Isabelle, from five years ago. "I mean, yes, I knew her, but I didn't kill her!" It looked like Donahue was about to intervene, but Ellis cut him off. "I didn't do it! Bobby, I'm being set up! You have to believe me!"

His partner spun around. "By who, Wes? Who could possibly want to do this to you?! What enemy could you possibly have that is so hung up on pinning these girls on you?!"

"Do you know how many perps we've put away over the years?! Is the possibility of any one of them seeking a vendetta against me any more outrageous than me actually committing these murders?!"

Donahue let the question hang in the air without answering. Every second of silence that passed felt like a spike going through Ellis's chest.

"Fuck you, Bobby!" He spat through his teeth, literally, as spittle left his lips. "I didn't do this, and part of you knows it!"

"I didn't think so, Wes, but the evidence says otherwise. You know as well as I do that you can't fight the facts, and right now the facts are all I have to go off."

Ellis tried to get to his feet in protest, forgetting he was handcuffed to the table. He yanked his wrists up, but the bolts connecting the bar to the table that the handcuffs were restrained to, as well as the bolts connecting the table's feet to the ground, didn't budge, nor did he from where he sat.

"Fuck the evidence! You *know* me!"

A pained expression overtook Donahue's face, but before the conversation could continue, three uniformed officers swung open the door into the interrogation room. All had their hands on their gun, no doubt in reaction to Ellis's attempt at ripping his restraints from where they were secured.

Donahue waved them off as they hovered in the doorway behind the detective in charge. Apprehensively they backed away, removing themselves from the interrogation room, but not before casting glares of venomous hatred at their once-respected superior.

There was nothing law enforcement hated more than a cop turned bad. It was not just a betrayal to the law, but a spit in the face of the brotherhood of the shield, and right now Donahue was right—all of the evidence was pointing to Ellis as the man behind this string of killings.

Chapter Twenty-Seven

After Ellis had been left in the interrogation room for another indeterminately prolonged period of time, the door opened. Donahue entered with a fast food bag from a local joint and threw it on the table in front of him.

"Eat up."

Ellis reached for it, but the cuffs attached to the table stopped him.

"This is a bit inconvenient," he said dryly, signaling to the cuffs restraining him from eating his first meal in over twenty-four hours.

Donahue uncuffed his partner from the table, but didn't release him from the handcuffs themselves. He then surprisingly took Ellis around the neck with both hands, leaning in closely. His hands tightened, but not enough to cut off his air.

"Pretend to get knocked out, and when the time comes, grab my gun, take me hostage, and get your ass out of here. I'll try to buy you time, and, if you're innocent, you damn well better prove it."

Ellis was shocked at what he was hearing.

"If you're not, I'm coming after you."

He then pulled back and delivered a punch across his partner's face, splitting open the corner of his bottom lip painfully.

"You son of a bitch!" Donahue snarled. "You've been a two-faced son of a bitch all of this time!" He punched him again, and despite the fact that Ellis thought he would be holding his punches, he barely felt it. He pretended to be knocked out by this last blow, slumping lifelessly in his chair as Donahue advanced on him again and kicked his chair out from under him, landing Ellis hard onto the floor where the wind was legitimately knocked out of him and his body sprawled out on the floor.

Damn, Bob, I thought this was going to be fake, he thought.

Before the theatrics could continue, officers burst into the room and held Donahue back, restraining him in the corner. A few of the other officers tended to Ellis.

"Get a medic!" one of them called.

Ellis was surprised they cared at all, but they probably wanted to see him face trial and go to prison, instead of taking the easy way out.

"Let me go!" he heard Donahue call from the corner. "I'm fine, I'm fine!"

The cops must have released him, because the next thing Ellis knew, Donahue had grabbed him again around the collar and was yelling at him from only inches away. Ellis snapped his eyes open and grabbed the gun at his partner's side. Everyone was suddenly five feet back around the grey-haired detective with their hands up in defense and apprehension.

Ellis jumped to his feet and wrapped his arms around his partner's neck. His hands were still cuffed together, so the gun was only inches from Donahue's head, cocked and ready.

"Back up!" Ellis shouted. "Back away!"

Donahue put his hands up and feigned fright. "Do what he says," he told his brothers in blue.

"I'm walking out of here, and none of you are coming with me," Ellis explained as he made his way toward the door to the room. He kept looking back and forth between the door to make sure no one new was coming, and then back to the cops to make sure none were advancing on him.

"Don't follow us, and he lives."

"Take it easy, Ellis," one of the cops said. "No one has to get hurt here."

"Stay there and no one will," he ordered, pressing the gun against his partner's temple.

Donahue squinted his eyes closed in pretend fear; Ellis could have sworn he even broke out in a sweat to sell the act. "Do what he says, guys. I have a family at home."

The cops stayed frozen as the two left the room, and then backed out of the building. They got into Donahue's car and Ellis drove away.

Once they were sure they weren't being followed, the two men relaxed, or at least as much as they would allow themselves to. Ellis could tell Donahue still wasn't sure if he was the killer behind all of this or not.

"Relax, Bobby," Ellis told him from the driver's seat. "I'm not the guy, but I'm going to catch him. You're going to have to trust me on this."

"I'm trying, Wes, but goddamn, this doesn't look good for you."

"It can't look any worse," he muttered.

Ellis pulled the car into a parking lot and ordered Donahue out.

"I need my gun," he said sternly.

"What? *I* need your gun."

"If we're going to make this look real, then I need to say I struggled with you, got my gun back, and fired off a couple of shots before you sped away."

Ellis sighed. He was right. He grudgingly handed the weapon over, and Donahue fired a few shots into the air.

"Now go, get out of here. Clear your name."

He still seemed conflicted about this, but Ellis knew part of him, no matter how deep, knew he wasn't capable of this, and that was why he was taking a chance on his partner.

"Go!"

Ellis nodded his appreciation and sped away.

Chapter Twenty-Eight

While he knew it wasn't the smartest move on his part, Ellis found himself breaking into the medical examiner's office roughly an hour after midnight. The building wouldn't have the regular doctors and staff members milling about, but he was sure there would be at least the janitors to be wary of, as well as the occasional employee or two burning the midnight oil.

Sure, there were cameras that filmed much of the facility, but the cameras on the basement floor were significantly fewer in number. There weren't many out there who wanted to steal bodies, or chemicals to preserve organs. He also knew the footage wasn't being actively viewed, only if there was a reason to go back and watch it. The footage would most likely be taped over by future surveillance.

However, just in case, he wore a black hooded sweatshirt he'd found in one of the locker rooms. He kept the hood pulled far down over his face and kept his head down.

He took the stairs down to the basement level. The last thing he needed was the ding of the lift signaling his arrival in the metal box before the doors even opened.

It appeared luck was on his side, as he didn't encounter a single person on his way down, and when he pushed down on the door handle of Oliver's exam room, it was thankfully unlocked.

He knew this was where he would find her. There was nowhere else she would have been, as Oliver had no doubt been placed in charge of the case as the leading M.E. Not only had Jensen refused to take any more of the bodies, the vics were more and more mutilated as murders progressed, and the police force saw Oliver as unbiased toward the detective in question.

Hell, after the altercation over Selene's death, it wouldn't surprise him if they all knew of the hatred the medical examiner had for the

They were all probably secretly hoping Oliver would
[...]ence in their favor to make sure Ellis would fry, guilty or

Ellis slipped into the room, closing the door silently behind him.
Adrenaline was pumping through his veins, so much so he didn't even
register the scent that he dreaded so much.

The room was dimly lit, but he was still able to easily maneuver
around the equipment and tables as he made his way to the back wall
of the coolers. Celeste would have been on ice for nearly thirty-six
hours now, and given the prominence of the case, he was sure Oliver
had already performed the autopsy.

He wished he could have said his goodbyes while she was whole
and complete. It was bad enough he had to prepare himself to see his
blue-eyed girl lying on the slab, lifeless and pale. He now had to see the
stitches that had sewed her up after the butcher had examined her organs.

He found the metal chamber with her name and information on it.
He paused hesitantly, hand on the metal pull-down lever that released
the door and pulled it open. He didn't know if he could do this. In the
silence of the room, he could hear his own heart beating, pulsing and
throbbing loudly in his ears. His heart was breaking, and to open this
door would make her death undeniable.

With a single breath through his dry and parted lips, he pulled
down on the handle and heard the door click as it unlatched. His hand
trembled as he pulled it back slowly on the hinges. He felt the cold air
greet his hot, flushed face, and until that point Ellis hadn't realized he
was sweating.

From this point of view, he could see just the crown of her head.
Even in the dim light, her hair glowed golden and ethereal. It was
beautifully smooth. When he had seen her last, she had ironed large,
wavy curls into it. The M.E. must have washed her hair while preparing
her for examination, removing the work she had so carefully put into
her appearance. No matter how she was styled for her upcoming wake,
Ellis knew she would have been disappointed by how they made her look.

The minutes ticked by. He didn't want to say his goodbyes like this,
in a cold medical examiner's room, where her body had already been
violated and was covered by nothing but a thin sheet. To say goodbye
at all was to face the fact that he had failed her. To come to terms with
the fact that he hadn't protected her, that he couldn't keep her alive, was

not something Ellis was ready for. Regardless, this was his only chance, and if near future events unfolded the way he expected they might, then there was a strong possibility he would be seeing his blue-eyed girl again much sooner than later.

He smoothly pulled the metal bed out from the cold chamber. It slid easily and caught on the track until it reached the end in a loud click that made the weary detective jump.

The sheet started just below her shoulders. Painfully looking down upon her face, she appeared at peace. Even her makeup had been stripped away, and this made her look even younger than she was. Clean-faced and with her eyes closed, she looked like a slumbering angel. His angel. His little masochist. His blue-eyed girl.

He placed a hand on the top of her head, feeling her soft hair beneath his palm, and a single tear trickled down his cheek. This was the one he would have done anything for. He would have quit the force, he would have bought her a home anywhere she wanted to live, he would have made all of her happily-ever-afters come true. Most of all, he would have waited for her to be ready to settle down and be his, only his, forever. To love him the way he now, and only now, realized he had loved her all of this time.

There had been something in her eyes that weekend at the beach house that he knew was different, and he had his suspicions that a change had occurred inside of her—a change that made her look at him as more than just a casual fuck. More than just her grey-haired detective. They had never got to talk about it and now they never would, but to have seen it in her blue eyes was enough to have given him hope that maybe one day, someday, he would have been able to call her his.

A second tear escaped him and landed on her bare shoulder, right above the Y-incision. He leaned down and slowly pressed his lips to her forehead. Her skin was cool against his kiss. Inhumanly cool. He could still detect a brief flurry of her scent on her cold skin, and the taste of her when he pulled up and wet his dry lips. This would be the last time he would be able to fully indulge in her essence, and his heart broke at the thought of it.

"I'm sorry," he whispered. Even if he didn't have to keep his voice lowered to avoid detection, he didn't know if he could muster more than this whisper of grief and pain. There was so much he wanted to say, so much more wanted to tell her, but it all got caught up, forming a

Ellis brought the blade to the side of his captive's face. The cold metal was close enough to his skin where a mere breath could have been enough movement to encourage the blade to kiss his skin. It was now apparent he had been holding his breath in fear to avoid being cut by the implement; he knew by firsthand experience how sharp it was.

"You disgust me, Ollie." The mere thought of him touching Celeste in her permanent slumber had him tightening his grip on the stainless steel handle. "You and your upstanding reputation and clean record," he seethed disgustedly, "while the whole time you've been fucking the girls that are rolled in here." He let his words sink in as silence filled in the gaps as he paused. "People should never look at you and feel that they can trust you again." He pressed the blade into Oliver's cheek and broke the skin. A trickle of blood quickly made its way down his face, where it dripped and spread onto the white medical jacket he had taken so much pride in.

Oliver grit his teeth in pain as the blade cut into him, and a pain-filled exhale escaped as the blade continued to move cross his skin.

Ellis lifted the blade momentarily. "When I clear my name from all of this, and I assure I will, you can be sure I'm going to bring you down." He carved two more lines into him as the doctor moaned in anguish.

More blood made its way onto his once-pristine white coat. The drops hit the fabric and spread out along the threads of the garment that held so much power in the community.

Ellis had made the capital letter "N" in his left cheek, no doubt for "Necrophiliac," a fitting choice for the medical examiner who'd desecrated who knew how many of the cadavers that were wheeled into his office each day.

"Until then, I'm just going to have to settle for this." For a satisfying punctuation to the end of his short lived torture he delivered a blow across the side of the doctor's head. Instantly blood spurted from his mouth, spraying across the wall of stainless steel doors he was shoved up against. The hit instantly knocked him out and Ellis dropped him to the floor, pants still around his ankles. After finding some medical tape, the detective bound Oliver to the pipes leading into the ground from the metal washing table.

"I'll be back for you," he told the unconscious doctor in a low menacing voice. He wanted to do so much more to him, but time wasn't a luxury he had at the moment. He would have to settle for the "N" he'd carved into his face that would no doubt scar and be a constant reminder to him of his crimes. Pity. There was so, so much more he could have done that the doctor deserved.

Chapter Twenty-Nine

Ellis knew where he had to go, even before he'd said his goodbyes to Celeste. Something Donahue had mentioned in the interrogation room had clicked in his head as his detective skills had come back to him through his muddled thoughts of nearing a breaking point. Fortunately, where he had to go had no threat of police or spectators.

Ellis entered the third floor of the warehouse where he had come so close to capturing the killer. If he had pursued them right then and there instead of attending to Selene, then Celeste never would have died, and this is exactly why the detective knew this was where he was going to find his killer tonight. These kills were personal—they were about Ellis—and now whoever it was wanted to rub the grieving man's face in it.

Shining his flashlight around the open floor plan, he saw pieces of yellow crime scene tape reflect back at him, the only real color in the room. It was wrapped around the pillar Selene was found against, and the tails of plastic ribbon fluttered lightly from a nearly undetectable breeze. At the base of the pillar was a large black stain from Selene's wounds. There was no need to have called the cleanup crew for an abandoned building, and her blood would forever stain the floor here, until the warehouse was repurposed or demolished.

He kept his beam of light moving as he examined the area, but it began to flicker and sputter out.

"Fuck," he grumbled as he hit it with his free hand. Each strike sent a momentary flash of light that immediately died. It looked like the signaling of a firefly in the darkened woods until it stopped responding to Ellis's forceful hits altogether.

A laughter came from the darkness in front of Ellis, and he instinctively reached for the gun that would usually be at his side, but not tonight.

Ellis heard footsteps advance toward him, small and light. The owner of the laughter came into sight as the overcast night sky barely illuminated the silhouette in the darkness. Slight build, slender shoulders, thin jean-clad legs. This was not the person Ellis was expecting. They removed their hood, much like the sweatshirt Ellis had been wearing in the basement just hours earlier, and a locks of platinum hair tumbled out.

Ellis gasped, recognizing the woman as Alyssa Kyle.

"Donahue said you were dead!"

She laughed her wind-chime laughter, the same high-pitched laughter that she used to flirt with him at her desk inside the office building he frequented so often. It now made him cringe in revolt, and, if anything, it now sounded more like a cackle.

"They saw what I wanted them to find," she spat. "Some blood, some hair, the overturned furniture." She laughed. "It was easy. Working with cops for so long, you know all the tricks to mimic a crime scene." She narrowed her sight seductively on Ellis and slinked toward him familiarly. "Not to mention getting the M.E. to draw a bag of blood to use for the crime scene in my apartment." She grinned, satisfied with herself. "It turns out your friend Dr. Jensen likes his women on the younger side. To convince him to do me this favor was easy. I just batted my eyelashes and smiled sweetly, giving him a line about how much I enjoyed older and more experienced men." She grinned. "You know what I'm talking about, Wes. It's the same line you fell for."

His head spun and he felt nauseated.

"Originally, I was just hoping the court system would have their way with you. Prison for a well-known detective is worse than anything *I* personally could do to you." Suddenly she drew a gun on him from the back waistband of her jeans. "But now that I have the opportunity to shoot you myself, since your moron partner let you out of holding, I think I'll just have to take it." A smile danced on her perfect red lips.

"You killed all of those girls," he growled angrily. It was more of an accusation than a question.

Her laughter returned as she threw her head back, her platinum hair animated wildly in the amusement of his realization.

"Of course!" she declared victoriously.

"But why?"

She composed herself and settled the gun back on him. Her voice was more serious now, pensive even. "I am genuinely surprised and a bit hurt you haven't figured that part out yet, Detective."

She reached into her pocket with her free hand and removed a handful of gold necklaces—all of the necklaces that had been worn by the previous victims. They swung in the air in front of her, tangling amongst themselves, but he could clearly see each held a lower-case initial on them. She then tugged at the gold chain from around her neck which held her lower-case "a" and threw the handful of gold at him, sending them skidding to his feet.

"Now you have the final piece of the puzzle, Detective."

The letters from all of the previous girls flashed through his mind's eye as he put them together into one word, now complete with the letter at his feet.

"Chasity," Alyssa said aloud for him.

Ellis felt the room spin. His head became light and heavy all at the same time. The mere mention of her name, a name he hadn't heard in nearly forty years, disarmed him. *This is what going crazy must feel like.*

"How do you know Chasity?" he finally asked, his voice weak and stripped of any authority he once had.

"I think the question is, how do *you* know Chasity, Detective?"

His mind flashed back over the nightmares he had been having for weeks now. The golden-haired beauty, the black satin dress, the forest. It all made sense now. His own guilt and past had somehow influenced his subconscious as he slept. In a way, his subconscious knew this was coming even before he did.

"We were childhood friends," he answered quickly.

She scoffed. "Friends. Right."

"How did you know her?!" he fired back.

"I was her sister."

Silence filled the gap between them as Ellis let the words sink in. His head spun, trying desperately to remember all those years ago. The girl Alyssa spoke of did have two younger sisters, but he couldn't recall their names or even their ages, just that they were quite a bit younger than she.

"That's right." She switched the gun from one hand to another, still aiming it at her target across the floor. "The girl you killed had a family. Or do you not remember that?"

"What?! I didn't kill anyone!" he quickly protested.

"You were there. Your hair was found on her, your DNA. Yet your daddy, the sheriff, made it all go away." She sounded revolted as she recalled the past. "I was too young to understand at the time, but over the years I pieced it all together. Piece by piece, detail by detail."

"You're right, I was there that night. I saw her earlier that evening, but I didn't kill her. I didn't kill anybody."

"Sure you did, Wes. You killed Yvonne, Selene, Tina, Holly, Isabelle, me…" She paused briefly after each girl, letting each name hit him one by one.

Each name felt like a cut into his soul, small, precise, and deep, that bled profusely. He knew that despite the fact he did not kill them, their blood was on his hands. Before he could continue along this self-loathing path, she continued.

"And let us not forget the last one. The *best* one." She grinned widely. She was just toying with him now. "Your love"—her grin grew wider as her face displayed mock sorrow—"your beloved Celeste."

"You fucking bitch! You don't even get to say her name!" he shouted, spit flying from his words as he moved to advance on her. He was ready to choke the life out of her with his own hands, and this time kink would have nothing to do with it. Just hate. Hate, revenge, and pure wrath.

"Hey!" she shouted angrily, pointing the gun at him and freezing him in his place. She took a bold few steps forward herself to demonstrate that she was the one in control. "Stay right there!"

He came to an immediate halt as the gun sight found his center mass. "Fuck you," he growled through his gritted teeth.

She laughed before her face went stoic once again. "We already did that," she spat back. "Remember?"

That sickening, sinking feeling returned to his stomach. He felt like his knees were about to give out from beneath him.

"Can you imagine what it was like letting you inside of me, knowing what you did to Chasity?"

"I didn't kill her!"

Alyssa continued on as if she was never interrupted. "Flirting with you, baiting you, leading you on to think that I wanted you." Her tone was thick with disgust and resentment, which her face mirrored explicitly. "And finally I let you fuck me in my own bed." She looked as if she was going to vomit. "Did you know after you left I showered for over an hour, trying to get the scent of you off of me? Trying desperately to get those images of you out of my head." He eyes slipped away for a moment back to that past memory, but before he could take advantage of the situation she was in the present again. "But hey, you can't spell Chasity without an "a," and it seemed more than appropriate it would be my necklace that completed the puzzle."

"You're sick."

"No, Detective Ellis, that would be *you*. The man who killed seven girls he had once fucked and played with, by means of his favorite fetish—asphyxiation. And despite the fact they'll never find my body, they'll assume you got clever, finally, and chopped me up into tiny pieces to throw me into a river somewhere. Soon after your arrest, they'll put it together that the women's initials all spell Chasity, and they will search your life for a girl by this name. Finally you will be fingered for my sister's death. After all of these years, everyone will finally know who killed her."

She's had it all planned out, since day one.

"Even though you'll be dead by then"—she shrugged—"at least I'll know justice will have been served, because I'll disappear and watch it all unfold from my new identity. Until then, I'll have to settle for being your judge, jury, and executioner." She gripped the gun with both hands to steady her sight.

"Wait!" He held up his hand, as if to deflect the oncoming bullet. "There's just one thing I have to know."

She looked impatient with his request. "What?!"

"I'm just curious… did you get all of that, Bob?" Ellis asked slyly as a grin spread across his lips.

A baffled look crossed her face, but before she could say anything or even pull the trigger, Donahue stepped into the darkened room, just off to the side of Alyssa, closing the gap between them.

"I think I've heard enough." He had his gun drawn on Alyssa, and with his other hand he clicked a button, revealing the recording device he had been holding to capture their conversation. "Put it down, Alyssa. It's over."

The woman who had thought out everything so carefully had been caught in a web Ellis had built. For years she had planned this out, killed people, sacrificed herself, and all to expose the man she believed to be guilty of killing the one person she'd loved so much. She refused to let it end this way.

"No!" she screamed savagely as she quickly spun on her feet and pulled the trigger, shooting Donahue in the chest.

Instantly he crumpled to the ground, blood already soaking through his shirt and suit jacket by the time Ellis closed the short distance between them. He held his hand tightly against the wound. In the short handful of seconds, Alyssa had turned and made her run for freedom.

The blood gushed through the detective's fingers, much as it had when he'd tried to apply pressure to Selene's neck wound not more than ten yards away. That felt like a lifetime ago as he leaned over Donahue.

"Don't let her get away, Wes," he breathed heavily. "Not this time."

"Don't talk," Ellis ordered him. "I'm not going to leave you…"

"Backup is on the way." He grunted in pain. A thin stream of blood escaped the corner of his mouth and betrayed the brave face he was trying to wear. "They'll be here soon. You *have* to go."

He pushed his gun against his partner's bloody hand.

"Go," he repeated, fresh blood trickling from his mouth. "For me."

He took another deep breath in, and Ellis could hear a gurgle in the back of his throat. He was straining hard to keep oxygen in his lungs, but from the blood in his mouth and the drowning noise that was now rattling in his chest, Ellis knew that his lung was punctured and he was drowning in his own blood.

Ellis also knew when he was being lied to. The line about backup was a lie, the way he had lied to Selene about the ambulance coming for her as she lay bleeding out in his arms. However, Ellis realized that if the ambulance was even only five minutes away, his partner still wouldn't make it.

Donahue didn't expect that his partner would buy his lie, so with one final shove of his gun he weakly followed it up with the two words he knew would get his partner moving. "For Celeste."

In an ironic turn of events, this moment, this place, was where he could have stopped Alyssa weeks ago before she continued killing. Before she killed Celeste. Before she shot Donahue. Now was his second chance to right the wrong he had made of letting her slip through his fingers once before.

Ellis gave his partner a stern nod and a look that reflected his friendship and loyalty to the man. The nod was returned and Donahue was trying with all of his might to not show pain or weakness. He clasped his hand against his wound as Ellis stood up to give chase to the woman who'd put a bullet into his partner's chest. He knew that, when he returned, he would not find him still alive.

***

Ellis ran in the direction he had seen Alyssa take off in. He hadn't heard any of the doors open, so he knew she was on this floor, hiding no doubt.

"Alyssa!" he called into the dark, still warehouse. "It's over! Show yourself!"

Only silence answered him. He quietly stalked the floor, keeping his gun in front of him at all times, and the safety off.

Suddenly a shot rang out from behind him. It whizzed by him so close he felt the air of the bullet on his cheek. The second bullet came in rapid succession, hitting his left shoulder. He let out a cry of pain and surprise as he immediately took cover behind a support pillar.

The sound of footsteps running from him came from only yards away. Ellis peered around the corner just in time to see Alyssa push through a stairwell door before he could return fire. He ran in the same direction and reached the door before it could close. He looked up the stairwell to see the platinum-haired woman making her escape. She heard him on the stairs and blindly shot a bullet down toward him.

Ellis took cover outside of the door momentarily, then barged back in to return a shot up the stairwell. She screamed out of fear, but he had not hit her and she continued her ascent. He fired another bullet, and this time it hit her in the leg. She cried out in pain and he took the opportunity to fire another shot. It also was a hit.

She dropped her gun and it clattered down the stairs, coming to a stop on the landing below her and above Ellis. They both looked at it momentarily, but by the time Ellis had returned his eyes to her, she was scrambling up the remaining stairs on all fours where she pushed on the last door that led to the rooftop.

The detective gave chase, only seconds behind her with his large strides. Entering onto the roof, he saw her barely able to stand, a hand pressed against a bullet wound that had grazed her neck, and limping off of the leg that sustained his first hit.

In the moonlight, her hair was wild and appeared white. Her hand, pressed against her neck, was wet and shone with blood.

"Are you going to kill me too, Wes?" she asked as he kept his gun trained on her.

"I didn't kill your sister, Alyssa." He repeated for the last time, quiet yet stern. "I'm sorry you think so, but I didn't."

She laughed, and it sounded like a mixture of disbelief and pain. Before they could continue, the sound of sirens broke through the night, and the red and blue lights from below lit up the darkness. Donahue really had called for backup.

"Let's end this," Ellis said firmly as he walked toward her.

"There's only one way this is going to end, Wes," she said quietly.

He pulled up his gun, chamber facing the air, and his finger no longer on the trigger. "I'm not going to shoot you, Alyssa." While he didn't necessarily want to save the woman who'd killed Celeste and shot his partner, he wasn't ready to pull the trigger on her as she stood there defenseless.

The sirens had come to a halt at the base of the warehouse, and they could hear the muffled voice of the officers emerging from their vehicles to enter the building. Alyssa glanced over her shoulder and saw she was close to the edge of the building. She took a few steps backwards.

"Alyssa—" Ellis took a hesitant step forward with his hand outstretched. "Step back toward me."

She peered back over her shoulder, the red and blue lights illuminating half of her face. The sound of the police entering the stairwell made her turn back.

"You'll get what's coming to you, Wes," she told him with an eerie calmness. She then reached toward her back and pulled her arm back to her front with what he expected was a gun.

Ellis spun his gun back around his trigger finger into a firm grasp and fired three shots into her chest. The force of them sent her stumbling backwards, and, in a mere instant before she fell over the side of the building, he saw that her hand was empty, thumb and forefinger in the shape of a gun.

Before he could reach out and grab her, she fell over the side, landing on the hood of a police car beneath. He walked to the edge of the building and peered over, seeing her sprawled out and lifeless.

Just then, the police entered the roof, shouts and yells of directions blurred together. Ellis turned to face them, and as he released his gun to fall to the ground, a cop released a shot and hit him. The detective fell to the rooftop right where he had shot Alyssa. He thought about the irony of it as his eyes closed and the darkness seeped in.

Chapter Thirty

Ellis walked into his bedroom. It was the first time he had been in his apartment since he had left it for his vacation to the beach cottage. That seemed forever ago.

Since the night he had discovered the killer was Alyssa Kyle, he had been interrogated dozens of times, yet not under suspicion or arrest. The recording Donahue had taken was proof enough that Ellis was not guilty, but the authorities still had to fill in the pieces and make sense of the whole mess.

When Ellis had awoken at the hospital, he'd been informed that he was a free man and no longer under suspicion. He was also regrettably told about the passing of his partner.

Ellis lumbered heavily into his kitchen as these thoughts passed through his head, still fresh and painful. He opened a cabinet that contained a few bottles of liquor. With his left hand, since his right arm was in a sling and cradled against his chest, he removed one of the bottles.

He examined the label, and the bottle which was more than half full of amber liquid. With a sigh he unscrewed the cap, held the opening to his nose, and took a breath in. That same sigh returned to his lips, and he poured out the beverage into the sink. One by one, he emptied each and every bottle from the cabinet into the sink.

He then slowly made his way across the living room to his bedroom. As he expected, his home had been ransacked, and his bedroom had got the brunt of it. His mattress was heaved up against a wall. It was gutted from end to end, with white mattress foam spilling out from the site of the incision. They obviously hadn't found what they were looking for. How could they? There was nothing *to* find.

From where he stood just inside the doorway of his bedroom,

initially frozen in shock, he moved his eyes to the open double doors of his walk-in closet. His toy vault, his collection, all of them were stripped from their rightful places on the walls. Now just empty pegs and lonely hooks remained on the walls.

No doubt his toys were sitting in the lab, waiting to be tested for blood and other evidence. After profuse apologies, he'd been told they would be returned in a few weeks once everything was officially cleared up. There was a lot of red tape to be cleared before they were back in his hands again, but he was promised they would be.

How could he go back to using them? They were an extension of himself, and now he wasn't even sure who he was anymore. The collection he once valued so highly and with so much pride was sitting in boxes, bagged and tagged, once waiting to be processed for evidence to convict Ellis of murder.

Some of them were decades old, the leather soft with use, faded from wear, and worn with the age of being used in dozens of scenes. Maybe hundreds, depending on the implement. How could they bring him the same pleasure they once did? They would never feel the same in his hands again.

He slowly made his way to the box-spring mattress which had remained resting on the bedframe. He was surprised it was still in the center of his room. It was probably the one thing that had been undisturbed.

Looking down at it now, he was really looking through it, reflecting on the past couple of weeks. He felt removed from the events that led him here; it was almost like remembering a movie—a horror movie. However, it was the demonizing of him, his toys, and his interests that was eating away at him from the inside out.

The more he thought, the more angry he felt, and it was sudden and fierce when the rage boiled up inside of him and exploded. The invasion of privacy. No, not invasion, the violation of his most private space. The manhandling of his most intimate belongings.

With his only good hand, he angrily overturned the one piece of furniture that remained where he'd initially placed, it until the box-spring met the mattress on the opposite wall as he let out a primal and soul-shattering scream.

Drained physically and emotionally, he fell to his knees. He was angry. Confused. Tired. Lonely. All of these emotions mixed together and flooded through him as he held his head in his hands. The murders, the betrayal, the setup, the deaths—all of it was too much for him and he finally sobbed. He sobbed for the girls who'd died, he sobbed for Donahue, and most of all he sobbed for himself.

Perhaps he was selfish for shedding some of those tears for himself, but regardless they came, and he did not hold them back as he embraced the emotions that he had been holding back for so long. His sobs were the only sound in the bedroom.

Slowly he lifted his head out of his hands, his right shoulder groaning with pain as he moved it back to the resting state it should have stayed in, and he looked between the metal beams of the bedframe that remained. Beneath, the wood floor was exposed. He cocked his head slightly to one side as he ran a trembling hand over the floorboard that rested in the center of where his bed would have been if it were still intact.

No, he was wrong before. He knew exactly who he was, and this is partly why he sobbed. With tired, aging fingers, he removed a loose floorboard from beneath the metal bedframe.

Inside the cavity of the floor was a small wooden box. He carefully removed it with his trembling hands, once smooth and soft, now aged with lines and callouses. His fingertips ran along the polished and lacquered dark wooden box.

With a soft inhale followed by a long sigh, he opened the lid on the brass hinges and pulled out the contents from inside the black satin-lined box. In the dim light of his bedroom, the decades-old lower-case "c" glistened on the gold chain dangling from between his fingertips.

The thought he'd had while on the beach with Celeste ran through his mind again. *You can only lie to yourself for so long...*

The End

Coming soon from Piper St. James

Stolen Innocence
A prequel to Stolen Beauty in The B&D Chronicles

Lying here in the woods, the autumn breeze played with her dark honey-colored hair. In the few rays of sunlight that remained, strands came alive, illuminated like liquid gold, bright and radiant against her cheeks. However, the cold didn't bother her, not anymore, as her eyes stared lifelessly into the low-lit sky overhead between the crisscrossing of the naked tree branches.

If the trees hadn't lost their leaves yet, the sky would have been blocked by a thick canopy of green, but they had long since descended to the ground. Now they danced around her on the forest floor, riding the wind in whatever direction it chose to take them, whether it was over her skin or getting tangled in her soft hair.

The rustling of the foliage was the only sound at the moment, but as night fell, the howling of the wind and the rattling of the branches would fill the woods. The branches were like wind chimes made of dried out old bones, clattering hollowly against each other.

Would anyone miss her? Would anyone even realize she was gone? She figured by the time the submissives of the household set the dinner table and her little sisters gathered around to eat, they would begin to ask, 'Where is Chasity?' or 'Where is Sissy?' Then her father would come through the door from work, and all thoughts of their older sister would be brushed aside as they took their places at the table.

It would be assumed she was in her bedroom or the library, it wouldn't have been the first time she was wrapped up in a book and late for dinner. A submissive would then be fetched to call for her. Where else would she be, after all, other than the warm comfort of her lavish home?

If it was any other night, her tardiness wouldn't have been tolerated, but when that submissive came back empty-handed from not finding her, an eyebrow would finally be raised. It was her birthday after all, and tonight her family was celebrating with her favorite dinner followed by cake.

Sugary treats were a rarity for her as well as her young siblings to indulge in. They were all destined to be on the submissive path, and cake was certainly not part of the diet they were all used to abiding by to get there. For Chasity to be late on such a special occasion and deprive her sisters of such a treat—well, it just wasn't like her to do such a thing. She knew her sisters were more excited about the cake than she was, and she would never be selfish enough to keep them from it.

But there was no special dinner for her tonight. No cake. Tonight she would be celebrating her sixteenth birthday alone. Not just this birthday, but every birthday hereafter. You see, she was now dead. Her body laid in the forest, not too far from her home.

She was dressed in her finest party dress, a black satin cocktail dress. Dozens of tiny sparkling crystals splashed along the bodice in whimsical patterns that spread from the concentration on her right hip and floated upwards toward her porcelain-doll face in waves of sparkles.

Her eyelids were painted in the gift her mother had given her this morning when she awoke—a vial of Blue Morpho pigments to paint her eyelids with on the most special of occasions. If her sixteenth birthday didn't symbolize a special occasion, she didn't know what did.

Her mother sat her oldest daughter at the dressing table in her room and gently brushed the blue iridescent pigments across her full eyelids. When she opened her eyes, she heard her mother gasp. Looking in the mirror in front of her, Chasity saw why her mother had made such a soft noise. The Blue Morpho illuminated her blue-green eyes, her most prominent feature. They appeared to come alive in an otherworldly glow that looked almost magical.

Her milky white and unblemished skin didn't need much makeup to bring out her natural beauty and youth. Her mother brushed a bit of diamond dust along her daughter's high cheekbones to pick up the light in the room in a warm glow, and then painted her full lips with a red lipstick that she topped with a clear gloss that made them appear wet and luscious.

Upon the completion of her mother's makeup tutorial, her father had come into her bedroom and presented her with the gift that she had long awaited since she was a little girl. With a proud smile only a father could convey, he opened the baby-pink box wrapped in a white satin ribbon and revealed the present inside—a small lower-case golden "c" on a matching yellow gold chain that she would forever wear until she found her Master or Mistress. Only then would this initial be removed and replaced with the initial of her Dominant to claim her as their own.

However, now, as she laid in those woods, this was the one thing that was missing. Instead, in its place, a collection of bruises formed along her neck. Deep, dark bruises that looked unnatural on the beauty's perfect skin. Her lips were slightly open in a small effort for her last breath that would never come, and they were still red and luscious. This was how she would be forever remembered on her sixteenth birthday, the year she officially became a submissive in the eyes of their society. Innocent, young, naïve, full of potential, beautiful, and with the one gift she had always wanted more than anything in the world no longer displayed proudly around her neck.

The End

About the Author

As a sheltered, yet academically superior 25-year-old, Piper found the BDSM community in her home state outside of the suburbs she grew up in. Stepping inside of that club for the first time is an experience that will never leave her memory. The chill of the vast rooms, the sound of the concrete floor beneath her high heels, and the scent of toy cleaner were all new to her. Being one of the youngest in attendance at the 21+ bondage club was intimidating, yet wonderfully exciting.

While she always had inklings that her interests were different, never did she speak to anyone about them. Not until she met her first love in college six years prior to entering the BDSM club did she ever meet anyone with a spoken interest for this subculture. It was then that the pieces all began to fall into place.

No longer did she feel alone in her interests, but never did she know a journey into a new world awaited her—a world that would soon become her own as she shed the world she grew up with and abided without question to learn to feel something she had never experienced before—empowerment.

Submerged in the BDSM subculture, life made a new type of sense, and it all felt right. Combining this new world with her love to write and create worlds both for herself and others to escape into, Piper finally found her purpose in life—to reach others curious in the real truths of the lifestyle from the safety of their own home.

Through written words, Piper enjoys entertaining and teaching readers about the truth behind the BDSM world without fluff and filler. Finally, there is an outlet for her to tell it like it is to an audience who is intrigued enough to pick up her book and read about it for themselves.

More Black Velvet Seductions titles

Their Lady Gloriana by Starla Kaye
Cowboys in Charge by Starla Kaye
Her Cowboy's Way by Starla Kaye
Punished by Richard Savage, Nadia Nautalia & Starla Kaye
Accidental Affair by Leslie McKelvey
Right Place, Right Time by Leslie McKelvey
Her Sister's Keeper by Leslie McKelvey
Playing for Keeps by Glenda Horsfall
Playing By His Rules by Glenda Horsfall
The Stir of Echo by Susan Gabriel
Rally Fever by Crea Jones
Behind The Clouds by Jan Selbourne
Trusting Love Again by Starla Kaye
Runaway Heart by Leslie McKelvey
The Otherling by Heather M. Walker
First Submission - Anthology
These Eyes So Green by Deborah Kelsey
Dark Awakening by Karlene Cameron
The Reclaiming of Charlotte Moss by Heather M. Walker
Ryann's Revenge by Rai Karr & Breanna Hayse
The Postman's Daughter by Sally Anne Palmer
Final Kill by Leslie McKelvey
Killer Secrets by Zia Westfield
Crossover, Texas by Freia Hooper-Bradford
The King's Blade by L.J. Dare
Uniform Desire - Anthology
Safe by Keren Hughes
Finishing the Game by M.K. Smith
Out of the Shadows by Gabriella Hewitt
A Woman's Secret by C.L. Koch
Her Lover's Face by Patricia Elliott
Love Times Infinity by K.L. Ramsey
Naval Maneuvers by Dee S. Knight

Love's Patient Journey by K.L. Ramsey
Perilous Love by Jan Selbourne
Patrick by Callie Carmen
Love's Design by K.L. Ramsey
The Brute and I by Suzanne Smith
Love's Promise by K.L. Ramsey
Home by Keren Hughes
Worth the Wait by K.L. Ramsey
Only A Good Man Will Do by Dee S. Knight
Secret Santa by Keren Hughes
The Christmas Wedding by K.L. Ramsey
Killer Lies by Zia Westfield
A Merman's Choice by Alice Renaud
Theirs to Keep by K.L. Ramsey
Line of Fire by K.L. Ramsey
Theirs to Love by K.L. Ramsey
All She Ever Needed by Lora Logan
Nicolas by Callie Carmen
Torn Devotion by K.L. Ramsey
The Story of JESS & AVER by K.A. Neeson
Theirs to Have by K.L. Ramsey
Fighting for Justice by K.L. Ramsey
Paging Dr. Turov by Gibby Campbell
A Thread of Sand by Alan Souter

Our back catalog is being released on Kindle Unlimited
You can find us on:
Twitter: BVSBooks
Facebook: Black Velvet Seductions
See our bookshelf on Amazon now! Search "BVS Black Velvet
Seductions Publishing Company"

Black Velvet Seductions

www.ingramcontent.com/pod-product-compliance
Lightning Source LLC
Chambersburg PA
CBHW022124170626
46808CB00002B/832